Theirs

Taylor had been the one for Hugh, the only woman who ever knew the feel of his strong, magnificent body against hers, and of those callused gentle hands exploring and claiming. From the day they'd met as kids, back when their relationship had been about kinship and understanding, through the sweet, sweet years of discovering love, then passion...all the way to the moment court bailiffs escorted him away, there had never been anyone else for either of them. That was a huge stack of memories for a woman to repress....

Now, fourteen years later, Hugh was free...and Taylor needed to tell him about her son...*his* son!

* * * * * * * * *

More Praise for Award-winning author Helen R. Myers:

"Ms. Myers never fails to give the reader a good solid, entertaining story with fresh characterizations and dialogue that sparkles."

—*Rendezvous*

Dear Reader,

LET'S CELEBRATE FIFTEEN YEARS
OF SILHOUETTE DESIRE...

with some of your favorite authors and new stars of tomorrow. For the next three months, we present a spectacular lineup of unforgettably romantic love stories—led by three MAN OF THE MONTH titles.

In October, Diana Palmer returns to Desire with *The Patient Nurse,* which features an unforgettable hero. Next month, Ann Major continues her bestselling CHILDREN OF DESTINY series with *Nobody's Child.* And in December, Dixie Browning brings us her special brand of romantic charm in *Look What the Stork Brought.*

But Desire is not only MAN OF THE MONTH! It's new love stories from talented authors Christine Rimmer, Helen R. Myers, Raye Morgan, Metsy Hingle and new star Katherine Garbera in October.

In November, don't miss sensuous surprises from BJ James, Lass Small, Susan Crosby, Eileen Wilks and Shawna Delacorte.

And December will be filled with Christmas cheer from Maureen Child, Kathryn Jensen, Christine Pacheco, Anne Eames and Barbara McMahon.

Remember, here at Desire we've been committed to bringing you the very best in unforgettable romance and sizzling sensuality. And to add to the excitement of fifteen wonderful years, we offer the chance for you to win some wonderful prizes. Look in the pages at the end of the book for details.

And may we have many more years of happy reading together!

Melissa Senate

Senior Editor

Please address questions and book requests to:
Silhouette Reader Service
U.S.: 3010 Walden Ave., P.O. Box 1325, Buffalo, NY 14269
Canadian: P.O. Box 609, Fort Erie, Ont. L2A 5X3

HELEN R. MYERS
THE OFFICER AND THE RENEGADE

SILHOUETTE *Desire*
Published by Silhouette Books
America's Publisher of Contemporary Romance

If you purchased this book without a cover you should be aware
that this book is stolen property. It was reported as "unsold and
destroyed" to the publisher, and neither the author nor the
publisher has received any payment for this "stripped book."

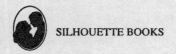

SILHOUETTE BOOKS

ISBN 0-373-76102-3

THE OFFICER AND THE RENEGADE

Copyright © 1997 by Helen R. Myers

All rights reserved. Except for use in any review, the reproduction
or utilization of this work in whole or in part in any form by any
electronic, mechanical or other means, now known or hereafter
invented, including xerography, photocopying and recording, or in
any information storage or retrieval system, is forbidden without
the written permission of the editorial office, Silhouette Books,
300 East 42nd Street, New York, NY 10017 U.S.A.

All characters in this book have no existence outside the imagination of
the author and have no relation whatsoever to anyone bearing the same
name or names. They are not even distantly inspired by any individual
known or unknown to the author, and all incidents are pure invention.

This edition published by arrangement with Harlequin Books S.A.

® and TM are trademarks of Harlequin Books S.A., used under license.
Trademarks indicated with ® are registered in the United States Patent
and Trademark Office, the Canadian Trade Marks Office and in other
countries.

Printed in U.S.A.

Books by Helen R. Myers

Silhouette Desire

Partners for Life #370
Smooth Operator #454
That Fontaine Woman! #471
The Pirate O'Keefe #506
Kiss Me Kate #570
After You #599
When Gabriel Called #650
Navarrone #738
Jake #797
Once Upon a Full Moon #857
The Rebel and the Hero #941
Just a Memory Away #990
The Officer and the Renegade #1102

Silhouette Shadows

Night Mist #6
Whispers in the Woods #23
Watching for Willa #49

Silhouette Special Edition

After That Night... #1066

Silhouette Romance

Donovan's Mermaid #557
Someone To Watch Over Me #643
Confidentially Yours #677
Invitation to a Wedding #737
A Fine Arrangement #776
Through My Eyes #814
Three Little Chaperones #861
Forbidden Passion #908
A Father's Promise #1002
To Wed at Christmas #1049
The Merry Matchmaker #1121
*Baby in a Basket #1169

*Daddy Knows Last

Silhouette Books

Silhouette Shadows Collection 1992
"Seawitch"

Montana Mavericks
The Law is No Lady #8

HELEN R. MYERS

satisfies her preference for a reclusive life-style by living deep in the Piney Woods of East Texas with her husband, Robert, and—because they were there first—the various species of four-legged and winged creatures that wander throughout their ranch. To write has been her lifelong dream, and to bring a slightly different flavor to each book is an ongoing ambition.

Admittedly restless, she says that it helps her writing, explaining, "It makes me reach for new territory and experiment with old boundaries." In 1993 the Romance Writers of America awarded *Navarrone* the prestigious RITA for Best Short Contemporary Novel of the Year.

One

"Jeez...look at the place. You really expect us to live way out *here?*"

As Taylor Grace Benning eyed the small town coming into view beyond the highway's exit sign, she gripped the steering wheel of her aging red Jeep Cherokee and struggled to keep calm. It wasn't the view that got to her, though, it was her son. No less than thirteen-point-three years old, yet he remained cranky when he first woke from a nap just as he had at three months.

You'd think I would be used to him by now.

Well, there was used and *used.* Besides, her nerves weren't at their best, and the hurried marathon drive from Detroit hadn't improved on that status, either.

"Come on, Kyle, you sound as though this were your first trip. So far things don't look that much different since the last time we visited."

"That's the point—*last* time we weren't planning on

staying. Besides, I was a little kid. I didn't know any better.''

Taylor eyed the extralarge T-shirt that hung on him like a parachute over a sapling, and his baggy, ripped jeans, and wondered what kind of emotional explosion she would have to deal with if she told him that he still didn't have a clue. She opted for a mild cold war.

''It's not that bad.''

''Right. Who wouldn't want to live in a ghost town that's been painted every gross shade of neon ever invented?''

Ignoring him, she exited Interstate 40, which went on to Albuquerque, and eyed their destination nestled at the base of the Sangre de Cristo Mountains. Kyle was right; these days Redoubt, New Mexico, was like a surprise streak of paint on an otherwise no-nonsense canvas. The salmon pink, canary yellow, peacock blue and electric white buildings that she could see so far were startling against tree-covered cliffs. After driving for hours along the flat, then rolling, prairie tempered with spotty vegetation, this shocking splash of color was unexpected, despite her father's warning that the town was attempting once again to reinvent itself. Aside from the fresh coat of paint, though, there was no missing that most of the structures were a half-century old and spare. No Frank Lloyd Wright or Taj Mahal creations here. On the other hand, glamour and grandeur weren't what she and her son needed at this stage in their lives. The challenge was to make Kyle understand that.

''Forget aesthetics for the moment, okay? Your grandfather's counting on us.'' She hoped the reminder would trigger his conscience. ''Once you get a chance to stretch your legs and take a better look around, I bet you'll see things aren't so bad.''

''Compared to what?''

''Reform school for one.''

''Not funny.''

She wasn't trying to be; she was thinking about what he could have—probably would have—had to look forward to if they'd stayed much longer in the urban hotbed they had previously called home. "Sorry, dear heart. You leaned straight into that one."

The young teen slouched lower in his seat and crossed his legs, further exposing a bony knee sticking through his torn and fraying jeans. Her only child was at a difficult stage in more ways than one. While physically sprouting into a man, emotionally he was light-years away from adulthood. As a result, when he wasn't bumping his long legs or those clodhopper feet into walls and furniture, he was pining after girls aeons ahead of his maturity and experience, or else hanging out with boys too reckless and angry for any parent's peace of mind. A month ago, when her fellow officers on the Detroit police force brought him home for the second time for offenses almost worthy of arrest, she'd begun giving serious thought to returning to the land of her birth. A few days later, a call from her father had convinced her to follow through with the idea.

Despite the dark lenses on her sunglasses, Taylor had to squint against the late-June sun, which was nearing its midpoint in the cerulean sky. But her eyes stung for another reason, too: having been away from the state for fourteen years with few visits between—and brief ones at that—the emotions rushing through her were as painful as they were sweet. As a girl, she'd ridden bareback across this land, slept under the canopy of this incredible sky, made love for the first time in this relentless heat. Once she'd made up her mind to come back, she'd understood she would have to deal with those memories, the old feelings...many things. But she'd hoped that she would be too busy to be susceptible to the "what if..." demons. Apparently those gremlins were more resilient than she'd anticipated.

"I sure hope Gramps has indoor plumbing," Kyle muttered, twisting in his seat as they passed a weather-beaten shack with an even shakier-looking outhouse behind it.

Taylor felt her lips twitch. "You know he does. You're just having withdrawal pangs because there's no mall." Thank goodness, she added silently.

"Yeah, and now that you brought it up, what do you expect me to do all day while you're working?"

"Count grains of sand and dodge rattlesnakes."

"I'm serious."

"All right, so this ground is more clay than sand. I'll still expect you to be careful about rattlers."

Her son tugged his Detroit Tigers baseball cap lower over his eyes. "Maybe I'll hitch a ride back home. Al Deaton said I could move in with him if I wanted."

Despite a sinking sensation in her abdomen, Taylor kept her gaze on the row of stores coming up. "What a delightful thought. Considering how infrequently he practices any form of personal hygiene, being his roommate would be a genuine treat."

"You know what, Mom? I live for the day you don't have a wise-guy answer for everything."

"No doubt you do. But you'll be an old, old man before it happens, *compadre*. Even your grandfather said that the only thing faster than my draw was my mouth. Deal with it."

Usually that would have earned her a reluctant smile from Kyle, but he was locked in too stubborn a mood to let her see it—a little trait he'd inherited from his father. To hide his feelings, he turned to look out the passenger window. Taylor didn't mind the break in the conversation, though. She wanted a minute to take in the view herself.

The town of Redoubt hadn't been "discovered" per se. It had evolved quite by accident when in the early 1880s Murdock Marsden's great-grandfather camped in the area as part of a wagon train heading for California. The topography of the land had reminded this ancestor of the area in Africa an uncle had described to him. A member of the small British contingent that in 1879 held Rork's Drift from the onslaught of thousands of Zulus, the uncle, through his letters, had made a lasting impression on Murdock's other ancestor. Enough of one to stay behind when the rest of the wagon train moved on. Enough to carve not only a town but a prosperous ranch out of the territory, which Murdock now ruled.

Today the sign at the outskirts of town announced Redoubt's population as 914, about double what it had been when she'd lived here. It would be 916 if the residents showed a fraction of the enthusiasm for her and Kyle's return that her father did. He thought she was worrying for no reason, but she had legitimate ones. In the past she'd made her biggest mistakes by assuming too much, falling in love too hard, planning too quickly, racing toward tomorrow with an energy that had bubbled up from some bottomless well inside her. No more. She wasn't the eighteen-year-old spitfire who'd raced out of Redoubt all those years ago with a broken heart and shattered dreams. She was a thirty-two-year-old mother of a troubled teenager. A divorcée who'd walked away from a challenging but promising career. And although she still had more energy than most people her age, she no longer took any of it, anything at all, for granted.

"Hold me back. Is that supposed to be a burger biggie joint? I don't remember that being there before."

At Kyle's mocking query, she eyed the yellow frame building with the green-and-white lettering on the window announcing Boo's Biggest Burgers. "Me, neither. But now you know you won't starve to death. And there's the public library," she added, pointing to the narrow red brick building next door. "While you're feeding your stomach, you might think about feeding your brain."

"It all depends on how long the line is to check out the book."

She groaned at the joke that had been corny even when she'd been a kid, and scanned the rest of stores that made up Main Street. Many of the businesses had been handed down from one generation to the next, and she could easily recall the names of their proprietors—Graham, Redburn, Yancy and Montez; however, there were a number of new businesses—mostly antique shops and art galleries—that were part of the town's turn toward becoming a mini-artist's colony. She hoped those newer residents would also be openminded about having a female law enforcement officer in their midst. Her father didn't seem to think there would be a problem—and that, regardless, he expected her to do what had to be done.

"We'll soon see," she murmured.

"See what?"

Jarred out of her mild brooding, she shook her head. "Nothing. We're here."

She pulled into the parking lot next to the low adobe building on the far eastern side of town. The Spanish architecture, which would have been taken for granted in Albuquerque, seemed misplaced in Redoubt. As expected, the town's single patrol car was there. So was her father's white Chevy Blazer. How he'd driven it here in his condition she didn't want to guess.

"Let's go say hello and get him back to the house," she said after parking.

"I hope he doesn't try to hug me."

It was all Taylor could do not to laugh out loud. "Don't tell me you've forgotten his man-to-man handshakes, too? You may end up wishing he still treated you like a kid."

They walked to the front of the police station, Kyle barely an inch or so shorter than her own five-eight. By next year, she would be lucky if she didn't have to look up to the feisty pup. Her heart swelled with pride as she remembered the thoughtful, kind boy he could be when not under the influence of his schoolmates, and how his grades once reflected his good mind and considerable talents. Hopefully it wasn't too late to get the old Kyle back.

Things just had to go well.

As they entered the station, a deep baritone called out, "There they are! Hey, what did you do, break every speed limit between here and Detroit?"

A grinning Emmett Kyle Benning hobbled out of his office balanced on crutches. Injury aside, the sixty-year-old still cut a striking image, although his dark brown hair was now mostly salt-and-pepper, and his face had turned ruddy from too much sun and an unapologetic affection for beer.

"Hiya, Dad." Taylor reached for him to give her son time to prepare himself. "You look good for a one-legged cop."

"You're the one. Damn, honey, if I'd remembered how cute you were, I'd have thought twice about offering you this job. The guys in this town are likely to look for trouble for the sheer pleasure of getting arrested!"

Taylor had heard variations of that line more often than she cared to remember over the years, but she knew her father didn't have an ounce of male porky in him; he was simply making all of the right noises because he knew she'd never been overly impressed with her gangly body and unremarkable looks. Although she supposed she'd improved somewhat with time, she didn't miss her son rolling his eyes, or how Orrin, her father's longtime "volunteer" dispatcher and drinking buddy, was suddenly preoccupied by an itch in the graying peach fuzz growing out of his chin.

"I don't know how you ever earned your driver's license, let alone became the fine marksman you are," she said, "when it's obvious you're as blind as a bat." She added a nod at his cast. "And what are you doing on your feet? Didn't you say the doctor wanted you in bed with that leg propped?"

"I couldn't very well leave the town fending for itself. But now that you're here, I'll be glad to kick back and play invalid. Who's that big lug you brought with you?

Maybe I'll deputize him while I'm at it and get me a real bargain.''

Kyle all but elbowed her out of the way. "Hey, Gramps.''

Her father held out his hand, and Taylor could almost hear her boy sigh with relief when awarded a formal, unchallenging handshake.

"You're looking fine, son. How's your blackjack these days?''

"My poker's better.''

Emmett threw back his head and roared. "Orrin—you remember my family? Taylor Grace and Kyle Thomas Benning.''

They were summarily reintroduced to baby-faced Orrin Lint, whose thinning white hair and near colorless gray eyes looked at the world as if constantly trying to figure out the punch line to a joke.

Although he rose—which did little to improve his height—and thrust out his hand like a trained robot, he whispered to Emmett, "What're they doing with your name? I thought she got hitched?''

"Divorced,'' her father whispered back through a stiff smile.

"Both of them?''

Her father's smile grew strained. "Say hello, Orrin. Then shut up.''

Still looking confused, Orrin shook Taylor's hand. "Sure glad you're here, Miz Taylor. But I am sorry our plans for your arrival party kinda fell through. Things changing the way they have, them new folk just don't know—''

"Orrin, what did I just say about flapping that yap of yours? Come on, Taylor.'' Her father took her arm. "Let's get you sworn in.''

Although Taylor couldn't be more relieved to skip a formal celebration, she wondered what Orrin had begun to say and wished he'd had a chance to finish. "Dad, what's the rush? Can't we visit a few minutes first?"

Her father glanced back at her son. "Kyle, can you drive your mama's car yet?"

The boy nodded eagerly—a surprise to Taylor, since as far as she knew he'd never been behind the wheel of anything.

"Terrific." Her father beamed. "Soon as we get you legal, Taylor, Kyle'll drive your car to the house for me, and you can take mine."

"Take it where? And why can't I drive the patrol car?"

"You can if you want, I'm just used to the radio and stuff in mine. I thought you'd like it better, too. In any case there's something I need for you to do."

As he spoke his blue-gray eyes avoided her gaze, and when she combined that shiftiness with his odd behavior toward Orrin, it triggered Taylor's suspiciousness. Something about this situation was suddenly not the cut-and-dried affair he'd assured her it would be during their phone conversations.

"Exactly what is going on? Dad?"

"Where's my Bible? Oh, heck, there's no need to waste time searching around for the thing. Everyone knows that once a Benning gives his word he doesn't break it. Besides, if anyone tries to say this ain't legal, I'll whack 'em alongside of the head with one of these tree stumps," he said, banging one rubber-tipped crutch on the dull gray linoleum. "Now raise your right hand and repeat after me. I—and state your name…"

She remained more than a little confused, but Taylor took the oath and became the first female police officer in Redoubt, New Mexico. For the next six weeks she would be the only active cop, since her father had been forced to let Lew Sandoval go only days before injuring himself. As she looked down at the badge that he pinned matter-of-factly on her Save A Vegetable, Eat Popcorn T-shirt, she experienced another flood of doubts. Had her father done the right thing? She didn't want anyone accusing him of nepotism. And why couldn't he have waited for her to change into something more suitable?

"All right, out with it," she said, accepting the gun he'd shoved across the desk at her. She began slipping the holster's belt through the loops of her jeans. "What's so important that we can't all go to the house and get you and Kyle settled?"

"Blackstone's out."

Taylor gripped the Smith and Wesson .357 revolver as though it was the only link between her and oblivion. The last time she'd come anywhere close to losing control had been in her rookie year as a Detroit cop, when she'd held her first partner's hand while an internist had sewn shut a knife wound over the veteran cop's eyebrow. This felt worse.

She had to lick her lips before they would form words. "Hugh's escaped from prison?"

"Hell, no! Paroled. About time, too. Damn Murdock Marsden for almost convincing the judge to throw the book at the guy. As it was he made sure several parole boards kept him locked up."

"What changed things this time?"

"Apparently the old goat himself. He didn't even show up at the hearing."

That was good news for Hugh...and anything but for her. "Surely he won't come back here. You said that Jane still has the feed store, and that running the place without him has been rough on her, but—"

"He's already arrived, hon. Got in around dark yesterday. I hear Jane drove her old jalopy to Albuquerque herself to meet his bus."

Suddenly it all made sense, and fury surged from a deep, dormant place inside her. "You sneaky, conniving—" She looked at her son now gaping at her. No doubt the combination of heat and anger was turning her face the color of a well-cooked sugar beet. "Kyle, go ask Orrin to show you around the station, please. Your grandfather and I have a few things to discuss.''

"I'd rather stay put. It's not every day I get to hear you cuss.''

Wise guy. He was right, and she intended to keep things that way. "Do it, young man. Now.''

As expected, he pouted, but he left. Taylor shut the office door after him.

"Now, Gracie…honey…''

"Don't you Gracie me. You're lower than a snake, do you know that? Sneakier than a roach! All this pleading to me to come back because you broke your leg.''

"Well, you can see that's true!''

"But you knew Hugh was getting out!''

"Who could say it was a sure thing until he got here?''

"Oh, you knew, all right. And you knew I would never have agreed to come if I'd heard there was the slightest chance of running into him again.''

"Listen, all I'm asking is that you go talk to him. Tell him that things are changed here more than ever, that the new blood in town sides with Marsden on just about everything. Tell him no way he can stay. If anyone can make Hugh Thomas see reason, it's you.''

"You couldn't be more wrong—and Kyle and I are out of here.''

She reached for the badge. Before she could unhook it, though, her father managed to shuffle around his desk again and gripped her shoulder, stopping her.

"Don't desert me. Hell, all of the old-timers know and respect you. They're glad you're back.''

"How can they? They knew about Hugh and I.''

"Yeah, and they remember your integrity even more. That will count for bunches, and they'll convince the others no matter what earful Marsden feeds them.''

She doubted it. In any case, he didn't get it. "I can't be here,'' Taylor said, enunciating slowly. Her voice sounded desperate even to her own ears. "I can't face him again.

What's more, I don't want to have to go through that—and considering what I did to him, I doubt he wants to get within a thousand miles of me!"

Her father gripped her shoulder harder. "Listen to me. You did what you had to do. Anyone with half a brain knows it's only because of you that he's still alive."

"Right. I'm sure he thanked me every day that he spent in prison." Taylor backed out of his reach and raked her hands through hair she wore almost shorter than some boys did. "This is a nightmare. What were you thinking? Didn't you realize what you were doing?"

"Absolutely. You needed to get out of Detroit. I needed to keep this town from rioting."

And for that he was willing to sacrifice her sanity. Maybe she could have managed somehow if there was only herself to consider, but... She pointed at the shut door. "What about that boy out there?"

"Aw, Kyle's gonna be fine."

Exasperating man. "Now you're a psychic? Have you heard anything I've said? You made decisions that weren't yours to make. I don't want my son exposed to gossip and heaven knows what else!" She didn't want to think about all of the rumors and truths that Kyle would hear. To think she'd believed their relationship on tenuous ground before. What a joke!

"I thought of a heap of things, Taylor Grace, and I made a judgment call." Her father stood before her proud and unapologetic. "You understand the necessity of those well enough."

Unfortunately she did. And, as a result of one she'd made long ago, Hugh had gone to prison. Because of another she had moved to Detroit. Yet another had brought her back here.

Her father must have seen the crack in her defenses. With a sad smile, he inched closer, this time easing his arm around her shoulders. "Don't tell me there isn't a small part of you that wants to see him again?"

"I've often wondered what it would be like to stand on the moon and look back at the earth, too, but you don't see me climbing into a metal canister and letting someone light a few million gallons of fuel under me."

"You're worrying about the bottom line, aren't you? You're thinking that you were never certain yourself whether he was guilty or not, and how that didn't change what you felt for him. Maybe now you'll get your answer."

"Curiosity is not an adequate motivator for something like this."

"Bull. So why'd you try to contact him after he was sent to the penitentiary. Sheriff Trammell told me that Hugh's attorney said you even wrote from Detroit."

"Well, if he told you that, then he also must have told you that my letters were returned unopened. I think that was a fairly clear message to assume the worst."

Her father sighed. "Okay, then. Let him take one look at you and maybe it'll convince him and his mother to sell the business and move on, the way Murdock and his friends in the chamber of commerce have been trying to coax her to do all along. Shoot, Jane's barely getting by. Except for Mel Denver and a handful of referrals from him, most of her business is from the reservation folks. Maybe that's been enough for her, but I can't see how the two of them will manage."

Taylor suspected he was right, but that only made her feel worse. She had to ask the question she'd only asked him once before. "Do you think he killed Piers Marsden, Dad?"

He took his time answering. "Hon, he was angry enough to. And if someone had done to you what Piers did to Noel, I could see myself that angry. What's more, a number of people considered Piers's death a personal favor. Remember all those rumors about what a creep he was?"

"That's not what I asked." Taylor was no more happy

to hear these evasions than she wanted to feel the familiar, dull pain in her chest. She'd believed, hoped, that she'd gotten over Hugh. "Do you think he killed Murdock's son?"

Her father bowed his head, a strand of graying hair slipping low over his forehead. "Yeah, Gracie, I'm afraid I do."

So did she, and that was the tragedy of it. It didn't matter that, like her father, she'd understood the anger that would have compelled him to do it. There had been a moment when she'd first learned what Piers had done to Hugh's sister, after she'd witnessed the poor girl's trauma in the hospital, that she had wanted to hurt the bastard herself. The difference was, she had too much respect for the law.

"See, another reason I have to get this resolved," her father continued, "is because people are saying that once word gets around that he's out, the whole place will become a ghost town...especially after sundown."

"That's ridiculous. Hugh loved this town and most of the people who lived here. He's not at risk of being a repeat offender." Unless he saw her again.

"I'm merely repeating the consensus of opinion." Her father gave her a sidelong look. "Well? Can you handle this for me?"

The sympathy in his voice decided her. She snatched his straw cowboy hat off his in-box and slammed it on her head. "I took the oath, didn't I? What choice do I have?"

"Atta girl. Now make sure you tell him that I'm not asking for him to get lost overnight. All we need is some assurance that he *will* leave. Soon."

Taylor handed over her keys and picked up his from his desk blotter. "When I get to the house, I'd better find you stretched out on the couch with that leg up, and holding a cold beer."

"Can't have any. Doc's got me on damned pain pills," her father replied as she reached for the doorknob.

"Not for you. For me."

* * *

By the time Taylor made a right onto Main Street, her stomach was churning and cramping. If it wasn't for Kyle, she knew she could easily have made a U-turn and directed the old Chevy for the interstate, she felt that much the coward.

Hugh. Heaven help her. Until minutes ago, she'd believed she would never see him again; she had buried the dreams she'd once cherished for their future. The news that he had gained his freedom should have sent her shouting with joy and relief...only, thanks to her father's explanation, there was nothing to celebrate, and everything to dread.

Somehow she had to keep her wits about her, do what she'd been hired to do. The past couldn't be allowed to matter. Nothing else could matter.

It was barely a mile drive to Blackstone Feed and Supplies. A left turn at Crooked Pine Road and she saw the metal building. The plywood doors of the warehouse were wide open, and as she pulled into the dirt-and-gravel parking lot she saw a silhouette of someone moving around in there. She drew in a deep breath to ease the growing discomfort in her stomach, killed the truck's engine and climbed out.

He was restacking fifty-pound sacks of range cubes. A quick glance to her left and right to make sure no one else was around told her that her father had been correct; this was a modest operation. There wasn't so much as a forklift to help with the lifting and hauling, nor was there that much inventory. However, as she got closer, she could see powerful muscles flexing and stretching across Hugh's bronzed back, and realized that he wouldn't have needed any help if the business had been larger. But then, he'd always been capable.

She didn't like that her mouth went dry again. After fourteen years, she expected more from herself, regardless of their history. On the other hand, theirs was some history.

She had been the one for him, the only one who ever knew the feel of that strong, magnificent body against hers, and those callused yet gentle hands exploring and claiming. From the day they'd met as kids, back when their relationship had been about kinship and understanding, through the sweet, sweet years of discovering love, then passion…all the way to the moment the court bailiffs escorted him away, there had never been anyone else for either of them. That was a huge stack of memories for a woman to repress, even a woman with a profession like hers.

When she'd pulled up, he had glanced over his shoulder and recognized the truck, but he finished stacking the last two sacks before he faced her. Only now did she realize he'd been expecting her father. It was there in the way he suddenly froze. Because of where she was standing, she supposed she was little more than a silhouette against the blinding New Mexico sun. But apparently there was nothing wrong with his memory.

Finally, slowly, he began to walk toward her.

"How the hell did he get you to come back?"

She thought of potential replies. Since they would all require a strength and control she didn't possess quite yet, she simply said, "It's good to see you, Hugh."

He stepped closer, so close she could smell salt, heat and man. Suddenly it all came back—the way he kissed, the care he took undressing her, how it felt to hold him deep, deep inside her. The memories struck like one tidal wave after another, until she wanted to slump to the concrete floor and weep for dreams and innocence lost. But somehow she remained upright, and met his furious scowl.

He glared at her badge and read her T-shirt. Sort of. Mostly his gaze raked up and down her, and she concluded years of incarceration had changed his tastes. No doubt he now thought her about as appealing as a telephone pole. It was only a guess, though; his sharp black eyes gave nothing away.

He finally settled his focus on her gun. "Is that supposed to be some kind of joke?"

"No. I just haven't had time to change into my uniform yet."

"So that's why you're here. Funny how social calls mean different things these days."

"Please, Hugh." She saw no point in hiding the weariness in her voice. "I didn't know you were here until fifteen minutes ago. I've only been back in town for about twenty myself."

She hoped he could find it within himself to ignore the badge and gun, as she wanted to. If only she could reach him on the level she once did. As once no one else could. How furious she was with her father for taking advantage of their past.

"This is no place for you." Bitterness and defeat chilled his words. "It's not going to be a pretty homecoming."

"Yes, well...I don't know about pretty, but one thing it isn't going to be is violent."

"You think that badge and gun will stop the inevitable?"

He was starting to sound as though he was heading for the gunfight at the O.K. Corral or something. She needed to try another approach. "Regardless of what you think, Hugh...I'm glad you're out."

"Then you're one of the few."

"That's not what I heard."

"Isn't it?"

His piercing, unrelenting gaze threatened to turn her into a coward. She suspected a scorpion sting would feel friendlier. On the other hand, he had a legitimate reason for the attitude. "We need to talk."

Once again he considered her badge and the gun. "While you're wearing that stuff? I don't think so."

"I'm willing to put the gun and badge in the car if that will help."

Something primitive flashed in his eyes. "You can take off anything you want."

"Is talk like that necessary? We were friends once."

"Friends don't send friends to jail."

"I didn't send you to jail. A judge and jury did."

"But you told your father where to find me."

"To save your life! To keep Murdock Marsden from ordering someone to hunt you down like an animal and kill you in cold blood. I won't apologize for that."

He didn't respond, at least not with words. He did, however, close the few yards remaining between them. The lazy, almost insolent stride gave her ample time to confirm that he hadn't wasted his time in prison, but had made full use of the gym. Beneath the black mat of chest hair, there wasn't an ounce of spare flesh on him. Every inch of exposed skin was glistening, toned muscle. He'd been something to look at as a young man of twenty-two. Now at thirty-six, without a strand of gray in his black hair, she had no words to describe him, beyond breathtaking. But, dear Lord, his face... The hardness and bitterness in those sharp, sculpted features were too much to endure. In his eyes she saw a man who'd suffered every day of the fourteen years taken from him. This was a man whose entire aura vibrated outrage.

It took all of her courage to stand her ground, and she couldn't deny a brief impulse to place her hand on her revolver. Making matters worse, when he stopped a spare foot away from her, she had to tilt back her head thanks to her father's dratted hat blocking her view.

"When'd you cut your hair?"

The question came as a surprise, but it was better than others he could have asked. "When I entered the Detroit police academy."

It shouldn't have been possible, but his expression grew more grim; nevertheless, once again he took his time with this closer inspection. He lingered longest on her mouth. Once he'd told her that she had a heartbreaker smile and that her kisses alone could make him come. Older and wiser now, she knew men said things like that to women all the time to get them into bed. But Hugh hadn't. She'd been the one doing the begging—for what had seemed like forever. He had turned her down each and every time because she'd been only seventeen then. Turned her down, although he'd said himself that there would never be anyone else for either of them.

He'd wanted to wait, and had shown the discipline to do so.

Until her eighteenth birthday.

Taylor almost sighed with relief when he again lowered his gaze to her badge.

"If you're a Detroit cop, what are you doing wearing that one?"

"I quit."

"Why?"

"Personal reasons."

"Must have been a whopper to throw away what could have been a nice pension." He slowly reached out and fingered the shiny metal. "This won't bring you anything near that."

It was unbearable to think of how close his fingers were to her breast. Could he see her nipple hardening? "Sometimes money can't be allowed to matter."

Hugh let his hand fall to his side. "I heard that your old man hurt his leg. Is he all right?"

"He will be in six weeks or so."

"What happened to Sandoval?"

"The town got fed up with his bullying ways. My father had to let him go."

"And no one else wanted the job?"

"I'm the most experienced."

That had him lifting one straight eyebrow. "How much do you have?"

"Too much."

As expected, that had him searching her face again, this

time focusing on her eyes. For a small eternity he just looked, and she knew he was reading and gauging, but she wasn't quite the open book she used to be. She did, however, let him see her regret…and that she refused to be intimidated by him. Neither emotion seemed to impress him.

"Qualified or not, you shouldn't have come back," he said at last.

Taking hope in the quieter note she'd picked up in his voice, she allowed herself to continue with what she'd come to say. "You shouldn't have, either. People are nervous, Hugh."

"Afraid the half-breed may go on a bloodthirsty rampage?"

She hated hearing him talk that way. Except for snobs like the Marsdens, no one around here had ever said anything derogatory regarding his heritage. Even now, she'd been given no hint that people's concern was ethnically motivated.

"Let's just say you have friends here who are concerned that you might have some form of revenge on your mind."

"Now what right does a guilty man have to think of revenge?"

She wasn't going to fall into that trap. But he wasn't going to like what she had to say next any better. "My father— The chief says he wants assurance from you that you plan to leave before anything happens that we'll all regret."

"Tell him not to hold his breath."

"No one wants any trouble, Hugh."

"Right. That's why you came to see me wearing a gun."

"It comes with the badge, you know that."

"Go away, Taylor. Get off my mother's property and get out of this sorry excuse for a town. It's not the place you remember. Maybe we were kidding ourselves to ever think it was better."

"I wish I could leave, but it's too late. I already gave my word that I'd stay."

He twisted his compressed lips into a smirk. "You gave me your word once. We found out fairly quickly what that was worth."

Had she thought him hardened? He was ruthless.

So be it. Let him understand that I've changed, too.

"Congratulations," she snapped. "Now you've proven that you can sound like a bastard. But the message stands. There's to be no trouble. Understood?"

"Oh, I understand, all right." Without warning, he took hold of her belt and jerked hard, slamming her pelvis against his. "You try understanding this. If you ever come near me again wearing that gun, you'd better plan on using it!"

Two

"**H**ugh!"

At the sound of the reproving female voice, Hugh released Taylor and slowly backed a step, then another, away from her. Only at that point did he feel it safe to face his mother. Only then did he begin to trust his emotions again.

As expected, his mother strode quickly across the warehouse's concrete floor, and with each step her worn cowboy boots sounded a staccato beat in the already throbbing silence. She had changed a good deal since they'd locked him away, and the greatest difference was that, like him, she rarely smiled these days—not that there was anything to smile about at the moment. Boots, jeans and a man's plaid western shirt remained her uniform, and as usual she wore an apron with huge pockets. At the store it was always denim, at home she switched to cotton. None of that had changed since she'd started the business. As for the no-nonsense German bun, it was still a standard, too. More gray than sable now, but it hadn't thinned much that he could see.

When she drew closer, he spotted the pinched quality of her features, noted that her eyes were shadowed with concern and disapproval, the once-warm hazel irises shooting off metallic sparks. That hardened her handsome face even more, a face already marred by sun and stress-etched fine lines. Since Taylor was responsible for some of Jane Thurman Blackstone's biggest disappointments and heartache, it was only natural that there should be no sign of her gracious businesslike demeanor.

"It's all right, Mother. I'm not going to do anything foolish that will get me sent back to prison."

Even so, she stopped a few feet from them and crossed her strong, tanned arms. "Exactly what do you think you're doing?" she demanded of Taylor. "You're not welcome here."

"I'm aware of that, Mrs. Blackstone," Taylor murmured with a nod that might have done double duty as a greeting. "But I have a job to do. Perhaps you heard about Chief Benning falling while doing some repairs on the roof of our house?"

His mother's expression indicated that Taylor's question matched her fashion sense. "This is Redoubt. Everyone hears everything."

"Then you know he hasn't yet replaced Lew Sandoval. As a result, I've agreed to take the job. I—" Taylor gestured to her clothes "—apologize for the attire. But I only just arrived." She added more gently, "How've you been?"

"How do you think I've been? My son isn't home twenty-four hours and already you're here. You're worse than a bad penny and rotten apple combined!"

"That will be enough, Mother." Hugh may not have done such a good job of it so far, but he wanted to handle Taylor himself.

Ignoring his quiet command, she lifted an already stubborn chin and scoffed at Taylor. "What qualifies you to wear a gun?"

Taylor lifted her chin, as well. "Nine years with the Detroit P.D."

"It seems," Hugh added before his mother could respond, "that she wants me to leave by sundown. Apparently my presence is making the citizenry nervous."

That had her fisting her hands and setting them on the hips that had carried two healthy children full-term. "How dare you! All of you! The law can't or won't do what it's supposed to do, so you bully my son? Well, it's not going to happen. He's paid enough, and then some. And for what? A crime he wasn't guilty of! Have you no shame?"

"More than you can imagine," Taylor replied, almost too softly to hear. "But I also have my orders. Believe me, I'm very sorry—"

"We don't want your regrets!" Despite standing a good two inches shorter, his mother shook a fist at her. "You had your chance, but you betrayed Hugh, betrayed all of us. Go away and leave us alone!"

For a moment Taylor looked as if she would ignore the command, try to reason with his mother. But suddenly something inside her deflated and those unforgettable blue eyes shifted to him. "I've said what I was asked to say. The rest is up to you. Be careful, Hugh."

As far as threats went, hers had been all but wrapped in cotton. If she'd been like that in Detroit, small wonder she hadn't lasted. But as he watched her walk away, Hugh had difficulty holding on to his sarcasm. Strange...the last time she'd walked away from him, the emotions that had churned and stabbed at his insides were clear and acute— disbelief, pain and an anger that had left him impotent and all but frozen for a long, long time. He wished his current feelings could be as easily defined.

Prison had indeed changed him, hardened and embittered him. If necessary, he could stand before this entire town and tell them all to go to hell. At least that's what he'd believed before Taylor had driven up here. But now...

Hell, it wouldn't take a magnifying glass to spot the chink in your armor, pal.

If only time hadn't been so kind to her. He'd always thought her a natural woman, someone not unlike his mother who had a no-nonsense approach to her gender, but Taylor was more feminine nonetheless. That's why it had been such a shock to learn she was a cop. Shapeless T-shirt and ancient jeans aside, she remained one of the sexiest women he'd ever known, her fine-boned, slim body always moving with an easy grace he knew she didn't recognize let alone appreciate. Lady Blue, Wind Woman, he'd dubbed her when as kids they'd ridden over the hills and prairies. He had only to close his eyes to remember her incredible hair back then, how it would fly behind her like a golden eagle's wing. How could she have cut it off? He didn't want to acknowledge that the shorter style accented the angles and contours of her face, and added a youthfulness and vulnerability that was echoed by her sensitive mouth.

Damn. He had to forget that mouth.

"Can they do it?"

He welcomed his mother's intrusion into his thoughts. "Anybody can do anything if they're determined enough."

"Then what are we going to do?"

"Ignore them for as long as we can. Take one day at a time." It was a lesson he'd learned while caged. Consequently, he doubted few people out here could match his patience. In prison there had been little else to do but wait...and try to survive. "Don't dwell," he said as much for his own benefit as for his mother's. "You knew my coming back wouldn't be easy."

"Knew, yes. But a mother can still hope." She glanced at the departing Blazer. "It wasn't fair of Emmett to send *her*. That cunning coyote never did play fair."

She hadn't always spoken with such resentment toward the Bennings. Once she'd treated Taylor, who'd been motherless for most of her childhood, as tenderly as she had Noel. Then Piers Marsden raped his little sister. Everything changed after that.

Fourteen years. Noel was thirty-one now, and although still single, she was finding some peace living in Arizona where she worked for a private foundation that helped women in trouble. Several times over the years she had tried to convince their mother to join her out there. So far she hadn't succeeded.

"Would it be so bad to move?" he asked, curious to see if his mother had reconsidered.

"Your father was born here. He's buried here. This is my home."

His father had been Laughing Max Blackstone, half Jicarillo Apache and half Navajo, a strong, kind man who had been the center of Hugh's life. A state road department supervisor, he had been killed at a job site when an eighteen-wheeler lost its brakes and had gone out of control. Hugh had been twelve, Noel seven. Their mother had just opened the feed store only weeks before, and suddenly what had begun as a comfortable life became a challenging one as they all worked together to make ends meet. There had been some insurance money, but their mother had tried to keep those funds for his and Noel's education. He'd made her use his share for other things because he hadn't been in a hurry to go off to college, not when she'd become so dependent on his help. There had also been Taylor...

Words couldn't explain the way it had been between the two of them. Kindred spirits seemed a flowery, empty expression, and yet from their childhood they'd shared a strong connection, an understanding. By the time he was graduating from high school, friendship and adoration had grown into an unbelievable passion, and the mere thought of being away from her—even if only until weekends—

had been unacceptable. He'd been willing to wait until she started college and his mother's business was solid to where extra help could be hired. But then Piers Marsden entered their lives and sent everything and everyone into a tailspin.

"That settles things, then," he said, turning back to the feed sacks. "You're too stubborn to leave, and I have nowhere to go. Guess we'll hang around and see what happens."

"What about Taylor?"

"What about her?"

"Don't try acting indifferent with me. I lived those years right beside the two of you. I had eyes, and there's nothing wrong with them yet. Will you be able to cope, to deal with seeing her every day?"

Just the idea of that made him feel as if he'd swallowed a plateful of broken glass, but he managed a one-shouldered shrug. "We'll find out that, as well."

"But—"

"Mother," he said with quiet warning. "Enough for now."

His mother sighed, and once again glanced outside. "I wonder why she never married. Did you notice? She's not wearing a ring."

He'd noticed. And his heart continued its assault on his ribs thanks to that brief but intimate contact with her. Thanks to a lack of female companionship over the years, he knew he would have reacted to almost any woman; that it was Taylor who had reawakened his sexual appetite had to be the cruelest of jokes. So was finding himself pleased that she remained single.

"We aren't going to get past this if we keep talking about it," he muttered. He flung a fifty-pound sack onto the new pile with a little too much energy. As it landed, the multilayered brown paper split as though it was the finest wrapping.

Brown oblong pellets poured across the concrete floor. Hugh swore.

His mother eyed the mess and nodded. "I'd better go make some iced tea. You're going to need some cooling down. Are you getting hungry yet?"

"No!" he snapped, glaring at what constituted several dollars of wasted feed. But he quickly checked his temper. "No, thanks. The tea will be fine for now."

"I'll be back in a few minutes."

Hugh didn't reply and didn't watch her head back toward the office. But once he heard the door shut, he walked out onto the dock—not in search of more air than was available in the stifling warehouse, although he did rub his forearm across his sweaty brow—to look farther down the road.

The Blazer was gone. For the time being. However, it would be back, and he and Taylor would cross paths again. For both of their sakes, he hoped it wasn't soon.

"So what did he say?"

The screen door barely had time to shut behind her, yet Taylor's father was already sitting up on the couch and lowering the volume on the TV. She looked from him to her son sprawled on the armchair beside him. Kyle's open curiosity made her wish he'd waited until she'd sent the boy from the room.

"Use your imagination. It certainly wasn't, 'Gee, I'm glad to see you again. What? You want me to leave town? Sure, no problem.'"

Her father grimaced and scratched carefully at the two-inch scar beneath his chin where days ago stitches had been. Fingernails against several days' growth of beard stubble sounded like sand being crushed under the sole of a boot. "Guess I deserved that, but can I help it if the suspense is killing me? Will he or won't he cooperate?"

"My gut hunch is that I doubt it. At the same time, he

doesn't want trouble. I came away with the feeling that if people leave him alone he'll reciprocate in kind.''

Her father didn't look pleased. ''That's not going to satisfy Murdock or his allies.''

''Then *you're* going to have to talk to Mr. Marsden,'' Taylor replied, slipping off the borrowed hat. ''Because I happen to believe that if the parole board saw fit to release Hugh, he has a right to try to start his life over wherever he pleases.''

She set the hat on the coffee table and retreated to the kitchen, as much to get a badly needed drink of something cool as to regroup. Being surrounded by familiar, nostalgic things helped.

The two-story house was an old friend, the kitchen still blue and white and in desperate need of repainting. No doubt the whole house did at this point, she mused, having already noticed the peeling paint on the outer walls. If her father didn't do something soon, the place was going to look like a giant dalmatian dog.

After filling a glass with ice and water and taking several deep swallows, she refilled her glass from the tap and returned to the living room. Along the way she caught sight of her hair. Flattened and damp from wearing her father's hat, it left her looking about as attractive as a wet rat. No wonder it had been so easy for Hugh to act so coldly toward her. She wished she could say she'd been indifferent.

''Mom?'' Kyle leaned forward when she returned to the living room. ''Is this Blackstone guy dangerous or not?''

Taylor eyed her father, wondering what he'd been saying while she'd been taking care of his dirty work. While it was inevitable that Kyle would hear of Hugh, not to mention meet him, she wished she could spare him any of that.

''I'm not sure it matters what I think,'' she told him. ''What does is that there are people in town who are afraid he might be.''

"So tell them to take a hike. You're the law and what you say goes, right?"

She couldn't help but smile. When she was in favor with her son, he was prone to think her too capable. "Police uphold the law, dear heart, we don't make it." She gestured upstairs. "Would you do me a favor and start unpacking? I need a few minutes to speak with your grandfather about business matters."

As expected, his expression turned wounded. "Can't I stay? I won't tell anyone. You've let me listen before when you discussed cases on the phone."

"And will again. Sometimes. But I'm afraid this isn't one of them."

When she was serious, she always spoke quietly, choosing her words with care to let him know she saw him, not as her equal but definitely as someone she respected. The gesture worked as it usually did. Although he didn't like being shut out, he pushed himself up from his chair.

"I'll turn on the TV, too, so you don't have to worry about me overhearing anything."

"Is he terrific or what?" Taylor asked her father. "He reminds me of me at that age."

"Lucky for you, he inherited his father's big feet."

Everyone groaned and Kyle stomped upstairs. When Taylor heard him noisily shut the door to his room, she slumped into the chair he had vacated. She shifted again as the revolver pinched into her waist.

Her father watched her, his expression growing sympathetic. "It was bad, huh?"

"You have to ask?"

"At least you're not bleeding externally. How're you doing on the inside? I see you resisted that beer."

"Barely. Since I am all the law that's available for the foreseeable future, I thought it best to abstain."

"I'm sorry, hon. This is some mess I'm bringing you back into."

Talk about understatements. "You have no idea."

"So he refuses to leave, huh?"

"Can you blame him? Jane has a business. He won't abandon her." She shrugged to indicate the rest was moot.

"Then you're right. We'll have to convince Murdock to behave himself until things change."

"I said *you'll* have to convince him." Taylor pointed her thumb at herself. "You know he's going to laugh in my face if I try to strong-arm him. All he's going to see is the girl who used to be crazy about Hugh Blackstone."

"Am I hearing this correctly? What happened to the sharp cookie who took on gang members in Detroit and wasn't afraid to face off a two-hundred-pound mugger?"

"Don't start with that kind of nonsense. You know it's an entirely different situation when you're carrying the clout of a huge department and that backup is on the way, than compared to paying a social call to someone who knew you when you were in diapers." She thought of the tough and resilient rancher who'd once survived a winter night in the elements after the fall and tragic death of his mount as he hunted a poacher. "Besides, no one tells Murdock Marsden what to do. If he wants Hugh out of town, he'll do what he thinks is necessary to make that happen."

"Well, he won't listen to you dressed like that, that's for sure."

How typical. When he'd been in a hurry to get her to talk to Hugh, he'd dismissed her attire as unimportant, but now he was a fashion critic. "Speaking of uniforms and psychological clout, what do you expect me to wear?"

Her father frowned. "Good question. I can't blame the town for being tightfisted with my budget because they're keeping taxes low in order to draw in more entrepreneurs. But it's embarrassing that we can't afford two patrol cars, let alone salary someone to man the office during regular hours. If Orrin wasn't content to accept that cell to sleep in as trade for his services, I'd be in a real bind."

No small truth there, except that Taylor suspected Orrin would be as happy to sleep at his desk if a cell was unavailable. What's more, if someone ever complained about the trade-off, no doubt her father's longtime sidekick would be camped out in one of the spare bedrooms here. Still, her question hadn't been answered.

"Lew used to wear what you did, right?" She'd always done her best to avoid any contact with the ex-cop who'd grown increasingly arrogant and difficult to control over the years.

"Same as me, a blue shirt and jeans."

"Okay, then...I brought along a few of my summer uniform shirts. I'd planned to take off the patches and wear them around the house, but will they and my jeans suffice?"

"Shoot, sure. And you'd better dig out your old straw hat from your closet. That sun out there's more brutal as ever."

Taylor had thought the same thing herself this morning when she and Kyle were on the interstate. The whole world was talking about the depleting ozone layer and the increasing threat of skin cancer, but in the southwest precautions had been a way of life for ages.

"I'll go up and get it in a minute." She would also take the scissors to a shirt right away so she could change. "I thought after that I'd pick up some lunch and, after we eat, head back to town to start saying hello to everyone."

"You take care of you, don't worry about us. We have a whole plate of chicken and potato salad in the refrigerator. I had Lola make it for that exact reason."

His consideration came as a pleasant surprise, as was the revelation that he and café owner Lola Langtry sounded like more of an item. Growing up, and even when she would visit, he'd tended to take advantage of having a female in the house. She didn't mind; she simply had wanted him to know that she'd noted it.

"Thanks. I was afraid I was going to have to train you before you realized I wasn't about to play superwoman around here. I barely have Kyle broken in. You'd require a serious five-year plan."

"You want me to really dazzle you? I drafted Lola to get her kin to move my things down to the back bedroom, so I wouldn't have to deal with those damned stairs, and you two would have more space and privacy up there."

Not only was that safer for him, but Taylor was touched by his awareness that she wanted to retain a bit of her independence, and her sole parental control over her son. But almost as interesting was the repeated mention of Lola Langtry. "Why haven't you married her yet, Dad? You two have been an item for...what? It's been at least ten years since her husband died."

"Things are fine as they are, thank you very much. In case you haven't noticed, we Bennings don't do so great in the romance department. Look what happened with me and your mother. Then there's you and Hugh. And we won't even get into you and Jim."

Taylor winced. She'd long gotten over her mother, who'd been an ambitious and restless woman who left them when Taylor was a baby. The last she'd heard of her was back when she'd first gone to Detroit and had played with the idea of reacquainting herself with the woman who'd given birth to her. It hadn't been difficult to track her down—Ruth Grace Taylor hadn't attempted to hide. By then a high-powered business executive in New York, she also wasn't interested in a reunion. Polite but firm, she'd made it clear during the brief phone conversation. "It wouldn't work out, Taylor. I do wish you all the best life has to offer, but you'd be disappointed in the morsels I have to offer. Seek your own destiny."

This second rejection had hurt, but not as much as her brief relationship with Jim Patrick continued to eat at her conscience. She'd never explained what happened, the whys, to her father, and considering what was inevitably going to happen she knew it was time.

"Dad, I need to tell you something."

He waved away her hesitant statement. "There's nothing you can say about that jerk. Any guy who won't even give his son his name—"

"That wasn't Jim's fault. I made the decision for Kyle to have only my name."

"Sure. Because Patrick was a two-timing bum."

"No, because he fell in love. Really in love and not the sham our marriage was."

Her father clearly didn't know where to go with that. "Okay...maybe...you two did put the cart before the horse as the saying goes and were forced to get married, but that's no reason to excuse his behavior with that...that—"

"Dad." Taylor sat forward, willing him to listen and understand. "I was already pregnant when I met Jim."

That finally silenced him. She could see him doing some counting and coming up with an answer he didn't like.

She'd been so careful, so clever, so afraid. She'd told so many lies. Before he found out the truth in a less sensitive way, which was bound to happen now that she was here again, Taylor decided her father should hear it from her first. Of course, he was a bright man; she could see he was already drawing conclusions.

"Wait a minute...you two met the day you arrived in Detroit to move in with your old school friend, Ally."

"That's true. I was about to jaywalk and Jim grabbed me, saving me from getting killed. One thing led to another and..."

Her father held up a hand. "Don't tell me details."

"I didn't intend to."

"But you were pregnant when you *arrived* in Detroit?"

She nodded.

"*Hugh?* Kyle is Hugh's son!"

"Shh!" she whispered at his outraged cry. Anxious, she glanced toward the stairs. "Kyle has to be told, too, but not like that."

Her father wasn't listening. His face diffused with color,

he glared at her as if she'd just announced she'd stolen a nuclear warhead and had it tucked away in their garage freezer. "Why didn't you tell me? I didn't have a right to know? You lied! You lied when I asked if you two had been...well, you know."

"I know. And, Dad, if you want to be honest, you knew, too. But I didn't come out and announce anything for the simple reason that the one person who needed to know about my condition refused to talk to me. Had I said something to you, you would have turned right around and told him."

"Am I missing something? What would have been wrong with that? You were a kid. You needed all the help you could get."

"Great. Then he would have done the right thing, even though he hated me. Do you think I could have survived that? Would it have benefited Kyle to have a convicted felon as a father? No, it was better to take Ally up on her invitation and leave Redoubt." Her old school friend's gesture had been a lifesaver. "As for Jim, you're being too hard on him. He has a big noble streak in him and he did fall a little in love with me. Enough to want to help me. But just as he realized he couldn't be the cop his father and grandfather had wanted him to be, he learned he couldn't stay married to me. A short time before Kyle was born he met Janet. I wasn't blind. I could see how it was between them—maybe better than I otherwise would have, because I had experienced something equally strong with Hugh. There was no way I was going to stand between them. Even as I was packing to go to the hospital to deliver Kyle, I told Jim that he needed to divorce me and marry her."

"And to think I believed you when you told me that you and Kyle kept your maiden name to simplify paperwork."

Taylor saw emotion work on her father's face and felt

another pang of regret. "I'm sorry, Dad. I played it the way I thought fair and easiest on everyone."

"Damn it, I should have known," he replied, now more angry with himself. "I should have. You were a wreck before you left. But I thought you were upset because Hugh refused to see you after his arrest. Then learning he would be sent away for up to twenty years..."

"That's all true."

"And the boy did bear a strong resemblance to Jim."

Jim's Irish background had been an asset, and had their relationship worked out, it's doubtful anyone would have ever guessed. What's more, his father's middle name had been Thomas. Thinking of the Patrick family, she felt a wave of amusement and sorrow; they had been a lively bunch to be around, and were disappointed when she and Jim discreetly met with them to admit their dilemma, and that they were divorcing.

"At first glance, Kyle did look like Jim," she told her father. "But all you have to do is compare his baby pictures with Hugh's, or have them stand side by side now...." She bit her lip. "That's why I was so upset when I first heard he was here. Dad, he's going to know the instant he sees the boy."

Her father struck the coffee table with his fist. "Good! I hope it knocks his feet out from under him."

"Prison did that more than enough."

"Hey, you tried to tell him, but he acted the stubborn mule!"

"And here for a moment I'd begun to suspect you were plotting to get us back together."

He did well at ignoring her gentle sarcasm. "One has nothing to do with the other. Only, what if I was? You two were nuts about each other. Don't tell me feelings that strong die easily?"

Her father was turning into a sweetheart in his senior years. Potentially a troublemaker where her head and heart were concerned, but a sweetheart. "Do you hear what you're saying? One minute you sound as if you believe he did deserve to go to prison, and the next you're aglow with the idea of a family reunion.'' When her father guiltily avoided her gaze, she grew more exasperated. ''Dad, regardless of what I think, my decisions can't be based on what I might want. I have to consider Kyle. He's at a vulnerable stage. How can I announce that his real father missed his birth and all thirteen of his birthdays because of a murder rap?''

''It would be a helluva lot more sensible than what you have been telling him.''

''What? That I'd made a mistake once that had nothing to do with Jim, and that I was sorry for shortchanging him? That's the truth.''

''Is it? Hugh was a mistake?''

''You know who I was referring to,'' Taylor said with a speaking look. ''In any case, Kyle has taken our divorce well.''

''Give him a bit more credit. He might take the rest well, too.''

''You're romanticizing things again. All he'll hear is that I lied to him—and that I've been a hypocrite because I've always been hard on him when he's lied to me.'' She exhaled as a whole swarm of possibilities spawned to attack her conscience. ''I don't know who's going to end up being more upset—Kyle, Hugh or Murdock Marsden.''

''I don't get a spot in this?''

''No. Because you triggered this whole disaster. You know, Dad, I meant what I said before. When Mr. Marsden finds out that my son is also Hugh's child, he's going to see a conflict of interest and demand you fire me.''

''Let him try. He'll have to explain why a cop I fired for excessive behavior is now a valued addition to his crew.''

Good grief! Was there any news that wasn't a potential land mine? ''In other words, any way you look at this, there are going to be explosions going on around here from now on.''

''We'll cope. You tell Hugh, honey, before he finds out from someone else. Tell him...and Kyle. They need time to get used to the idea before the rest of the community hears about them.''

Taylor saw a bigger hurdle. ''You swore me in, Dad. Redoubt might not have the crime ratio of Detroit, but I have a responsibility to this community. The first thing I need to do is to get downtown and reassure everyone that there's someone on the job. The rest has waited thirteen-plus years. It will have to wait a few more days.''

It had to.

Her father considered that. ''I see your point...and for your sake I hope you have the time, but hurry, Gracie. If either Hugh or Kyle hear about this first, it might cause a break between you—''

Before he could finish there was a slam and a crash upstairs. Both Taylor and her father were startled by the violent sound. Taylor recovered first and hurried upstairs.

''Kyle? Are you okay? Kyle?'' His bedroom door was locked. There was no sound coming from beyond the thin plywood, either. ''Kyle! I need to know you're in there, son, otherwise I'm going to have to force the lock.''

''Taylor...you'd better get down here!'' her father called from below.

Something in his voice told her that there was a good reason to put off forcing her way inside. Wondering what else would go wrong today, she hurried downstairs to see that her father had hobbled to the dinette window.

He pointed. ''Look.''

Taylor crossed to him and saw her son racing down the road, heading toward town as if a pack of ravenous wild dogs was chasing him. ''Heaven help me,'' she breathed. ''He heard.''

''He's your son all right, Gracie. You used to be a grade-A sneak, too.''

Did she need this? "Where do you think he's going?" she asked, already retracing her steps to get the car keys she'd thrown onto the coffee table along with the hat.

"If I was thirteen and had finally found out who my father was...?"

Taylor didn't wait to hear more, she simply burst out the kitchen door and ran for her father's truck.

Three

"It wasn't the smartest thing you could do. But at the
same time I don't blame you. That rooster deserved becoming soup."

Hugh attached Esmerelda Calderone's loading receipt to
the clipboard on the wall and reached for a brown grocery
sack sturdy enough to hold five pounds of chicken scratch.
He began scooping from the larger bins framing both sides
of the warehouse doors, while trying to shut out the feeble
crone's voice. She might be only their fourth customer of
the day, but at the same time she was the fourth to think
she had a right to comment upon his return to Redoubt.

"You were always a good boy, Hugh Blackstone. And
everyone knows who was the bad *hombre* when young
Marsden died. Bad, bad blood in that one."

Hugh kept measuring and scooping. Before long the sun
was going to be inching into the warehouse, and the tem-
peratures would climb high enough to slow-bake his
brains. He hoped the humpbacked woman was gone by

then, otherwise he couldn't guarantee to hold his tongue. As it was, he was tempted to tell her that she should save her breath because he didn't give a damn what anyone thought anymore.

"How are your grandsons, Mrs. C.?" If he couldn't stop her one way, at least he could redirect her focus.

She raised an arm that was almost as thin as the handle on the push broom he'd set aside to wait on her. "Eiyeeee. Little Manuel is wonderful. He's with the archdiocese in Philadelphia. Can you believe that? My Emilio's firstborn becoming an important man in the church. As for Roberto—" her expression grew more whimsical "—he's now Mr. Rob at the Crimson Curl in San Francisco and paints people's hair purple and green. A strange boy. I think maybe chickens are easier to raise."

She could say that again. Hugh didn't weigh the sack he'd filled almost full. It would register way over, but he knew the old woman lived on social security and what her kids could afford to give her on the side, so he simply taped the sack as though that was normal procedure. Maybe Blackstone Feed and Supplies would go bankrupt, but it wouldn't be as a result of giving away a few cents worth of extra grain.

"That should fix you up. Let me put this into your truck, and I'll help you off the dock," he told her.

After setting her purchase on the front seat of the dilapidated vehicle, he took hold of the crone's tiny waist and lifted her from the concrete platform. She tittered like a schoolgirl as she hurried into the truck, her dark eyes twinkling with delight.

"Be careful driving home!" he said, standing back to escape being swiped by the closing door.

"Hmph. Been driving for sixty-three years. Should know the way by now."

No doubt, but she'd never gone more than ten miles per hour, Hugh thought as she inched the old relic away from the dock. As he wondered how many people had suffered wrecks or nervous breakdowns from driving behind her, he raised a hand in answer to her wave into her sideview mirror.

Once she was onto the street, he leapt back onto the dock and reached around the corner into the shade for his tea. Although he'd drunk most of it before Mrs. Calderone had arrived, some ice remained. Grateful for anything cool, he sucked one of the smooth cubes into his mouth and chewed.

Across the road at Redoubt Wrecker and Salvage, Tito Hernandez's rottweiler lay just inside the teetering garage watching him. After little more than twenty-four hours, the beast seemed to have decided that unless Tito drew a customer worth mauling, *he* would be its dinner...or breakfast. The dog didn't look concerned as to which it would be, and it reminded Hugh of the warden's companion back at the prison. He'd made a friend of Bull's-eye, and he would have Tito, Jr., sneaking over for snacks before long. But not today.

Sucking another cube into his mouth, he glanced down the road. A boy was jogging. Hugh frowned at the mere idea of that. Not only was this street, tucked behind the majority of businesses and hunkering in the shadow of the mountains, not the kind of place for that kind of thing, but it was the worst time of day for excessive exercise. Nevertheless, the kid sure seemed in a hurry to make time.

A new face, he mused, narrowing his eyes against the heat and glare, but in a way so was he. In any case, the kid wasn't used to this sunbaked sandy ground.

As if some invisible gremlin heard that and wanted to prove the point, the young teen stumbled. Hugh felt an unfamiliar urge to smile, remembering how, while growing up, his big feet had outpaced his body. Skinny arms flailed, but to his credit the kid ultimately regained his balance. The rottweiler had also spotted the boy. Fortunately for the kid, he angled toward their potholed parking area.

Hugh hoped he was coming to buy something and not

to ask for a job. As he eyed the baseball cap—his Detroit Tigers baseball cap—a tiny voice told him that wasn't likely.

As the emblem on the hat registered, something jarred loose inside Hugh, something that upset his breathing. When the boy stopped only feet from the dock and hunkered over to rest his hands on his knees, Hugh found himself echoing the boy's gasps.

"You okay, kid?" he managed to ask.

The boy took the hemmed edge of his black T-shirt and wiped at his sweaty face. The shirt bore no slogan and was big enough for three kids his size. "Stinkin' hot," he gasped.

"That it is. But most people know better than to move faster than a slug during this time of day. You running to or from something?"

"Depends."

Before either of them could say more, the sound of a racing car caught their attention. Hugh recognized Emmett's Blazer again; the truck kicked up considerable dust as it swung into the parking lot, and it came as no surprise to see that Taylor was the driver. She wasn't wearing the hat this time, and she looked about as upset as he'd ever seen her.

"Get in," she said to the teen through the opened passenger window.

The kid took in another deep breath and shook his head.

"We'll talk. I'll explain everything. Just get in."

Instead, the boy looked from her to him. Hugh saw his speculation and his own intensified, leaving an increasingly unpleasant feeling in the pit of his stomach.

"What's going on, Taylor?" Granted, she represented the law now, but this was his mother's property. He figured he had a right to ask.

She ignored him. "Kyle. You don't know what you're doing."

"Is that him?" When she didn't reply, the boy turned

to squint up at him. "Mister...are you Hugh Thomas Blackstone?"

Taylor shifted into park and sprang out of the Blazer. For his part, Hugh didn't take his eyes off the boy. It was impossible now. Something about the kid was awfully, awfully familiar. His racing mind was putting a great number of two-and-twos together, but he also kept rejecting the conclusion he kept coming to.

"I'm Blackstone." He felt much as he had the last time he heard the locks trigger on his cell. "Who are you?"

"Kyle!" Taylor circled the truck and grabbed the boy by his arm.

He wrestled free. "I'm Kyle Thomas Benning. Does that mean anything to you?"

Hugh wanted to sit down. He wanted to back into the shade of the warehouse and pull the doors shut. To hide and block out reality. Even the ice cubes he'd chewed and swallowed threatened to try for a hasty exit.

Kyle Thomas. *Thomas.* Shaking his head, he focused on Taylor. "What the hell is this?"

"I didn't know you'd been released, okay?" she snapped, before saying to her son, "Kyle, for the love of heaven, get in the truck and let's go back to the house. I promise we can—"

"This is *your* boy...?" Hugh had almost convinced himself that the kid was a brother or nephew or something. Stupid, but necessary. He didn't think his brain could handle what his instincts were telling him.

"Is he my father?" the boy yelled before she could answer.

Taylor closed her eyes, but Hugh didn't need to see them at that point. The words were enough, the boy himself was enough.

A son. He had a son.

He stared at the boy. Suddenly he understood the odd feelings. They were a sense of nagging familiarity and why? Because he was looking at himself, himself at...what? Fourteen? He did some quick math and realized that couldn't be possible. Thirteen. Yes! He was looking at himself at thirteen.

"Oh God," he whispered.

The boy looked plenty rattled, too—also betrayed, angry and disappointed. Hugh didn't blame him a bit, for any of it.

Taylor was the first to recover. She opened the passenger door and took hold of her son's arm again, this time more gently. "Breathe, Kyle. Kyle? Breathe. Now. And get in."

"Wait a minute." Hugh stepped forward. "I have a few questions of my own."

"Later."

After she closed the Blazer's door behind the dazed boy, she started back around the truck. Hugh used her path to his advantage and leapt off the dock to block her way.

"You can't just take off after an announcement like that."

"Watch me." She met his hard stare with one of her own. "Whatever his paternity is, he's *my* son first and foremost. I gave birth to him. I raised him."

"Obviously. But that's not the point. You kept him a secret!"

"You didn't want to know!"

Her fury was such that when she pulled free, he had to let her go. How could he not? She was right. He'd shut down on her back then, shut her out because he'd been so angry that she'd told her father where he'd been hiding the night Murdock was hunting for him. All he could see at the time was her betrayal. It had blinded him to everything else. Now he stared as she hurried into the truck and started the engine, stared as she sped away leaving him nothing but grit and dust, which filled the air and clung to his sweating torso, his face, and threatened to choke him in an entirely different but equally terminal way. He stared because he didn't know what else to do.

* * *

"He didn't know." Twisting in his seat, Kyle struggled to see out the dust-coated back window. Finally, as they turned left at Main Street, he swung around to face his mother. "It's true that he didn't know about me."

His accusatory tone echoed Hugh's, and Taylor gripped the steering wheel trying to find a note of calm so she could reply, but all she could do was remember the shock and pain in Hugh's eyes. "No," she said, her voice a thin whisper. "I left Redoubt right after he was— Right after he went away."

"Go ahead and say it. I heard you and Gramps talking. He's a convict. A murderer!"

She couldn't bear the way he all but spat out the words, let alone what he must be thinking. "They never proved that, Kyle. He was convicted on circumstantial evidence."

"But you believe he did it!"

Until Hugh admitted to the crime himself, a part of her would always cling to the hope that he was innocent, even though her logical, rational side had to assume he wasn't. "Look...fourteen years ago his sister was raped, and he fought with the man who did it. Later the man was found dead from a gunshot wound. The handgun was found in Hugh's truck, and even though his fingerprints weren't on it, nor could they prove that it belonged to him, a jury found him guilty."

Kyle remained silent for several seconds, his young face troubled. "Did he deny it?"

"No. He didn't confess, either. He refused to say anything, particularly to me. I tried to contact him a number of times, but he refused."

"Why?"

"Because when they were searching for him, I told your grandfather where he was probably hiding. Don't look at me like that." She groaned, shaking her head. "If Piers Marsden's father's men had found him first, he would never have been around to stand trial. Would that have been better?''

"Jeez...I don't know.''

Neither did she. That was the bitter pill she'd had to swallow every day since her decision.

"Well, no matter what,'' Kyle said after a short while, "you were wrong about lying to me all these years. And you were wrong to lie to Gramps.''

Oh, boy... Taylor nodded, accepting that old adage about everything having a season. This was hers to walk on broken glass and hot coals.

"Hindsight being what it is, maybe you're right. Then again, it's always easier to play armchair quarterback.''

"We're talking about my life, Mom.''

"That's right, *son*. Your life, which I protected the best way I knew how!''

Kyle sunk deeper into his seat, his arms crossed tightly over his chest. He didn't speak again.

Back at the house, they found Emmett on the couch, his hair looking as though he'd had his hands in it for a good while. When he saw them, he uttered a relieved sigh. "You two come sit down for a minute and try not to say something stupid.''

"You're too late for that,'' Taylor replied.

Kyle shot her a resentful look, but at least he dropped into the chair he'd been sitting in before.

"Guess the good news is that no one's bleeding yet,'' her father drawled, studying the boy's mutinous expression. "You'd better go on and say what's on your mind. No sense locking it in and turning it into something else later on.''

"How could you not know?'' Kyle demanded. "I saw him. I look just like him.''

His tone was slightly less belligerent than it had been while addressing her, but Taylor took little comfort in that.

"Well, I've been sitting here berating myself for the same thing,'' her father replied. "I shouldn't have turned a blind eye to it all because I know firsthand how tough it is to raise a child on your own. But I did that to your mother. We all—all of us involved—let her. And she was only a kid herself. If you're thinking of staying all puffed at her, you consider what it took for her to go to school, make a living and make a good home for you.''

"I didn't ask to be born.''

Like a phantom echo, Taylor heard herself saying those words to her father during one of the few times they'd fought. The crazy thing was, she couldn't remember what it was they'd fought over.

The two of them exchanged glances. "You're right. Payback is hell,'' she muttered, shrugging at his anguished look. Then she withdrew to the kitchen for a drink of water. She needed a moment to deal with this latest blow. Instead, her thoughts turned to Hugh.

He had been so shocked, so hurt, when he'd seen Kyle and realized the truth. Clearly he'd forgotten how the last time they'd made love they hadn't used protection. But that was understandable, since it had happened the evening of Noel's rape. He had returned from the hospital in Albuquerque, while his mother had remained with his sister. They'd had his house to themselves, and she had tried to get him to eat dinner, to get him to talk to her. So many dark emotions had been boiling inside him, she'd done the only thing she could think of to get his mind off them— she'd offered herself as an emotional outlet. She'd seduced him, willing him to do something beautiful with the energy his fury had spawned.

As she stared out of the kitchen window up at the mountains, she relived that last all-too-brief episode...how she'd followed him to his bedroom, stepped behind him as he'd stood by his window. Dusk had shadowed everything. She'd wrapped her arms around his waist and pressed her cheek to his back, broad and strong even then. Never would she forget his tension, or the way he sucked in his breath at her first touch.

Spinning around, he'd held her tightly against him. "Help me," he'd whispered, his voice raw and completely unlike anything she was used to hearing. "Make me block out the thoughts and images. Make the pain stop."

He hadn't been asking for sex, just escape from his own mind. Nevertheless, she'd given him everything that her heart and body was capable of. It had been the easiest choice she'd ever made.

Taylor closed her eyes and relived the sensations—the feel of his hands and mouth on her. Her body grew warm, her breasts grew taut as though filling with milk, her nipples became hard, almost painfully so...and, inevitably, an ache began deep in her womb where once Hugh had filled her, where once he had burned hot and hard.

Insanity.

She pushed away from the sink and returned to the living room. She heard the low but harsh buzz of male conversation warning her that Kyle remained angry.

"Aw, what're you bellyaching for, son?" her father said. "What Hugh Blackstone is or isn't doesn't have anything to do with who you've grown to be."

"Yes, it does! And I have a right to figure out what I think about that."

"You're right, you do," Taylor said, perching on the arm of the sofa. "But please take your time. In fact, it might help if you let yourself sleep on it a day or two."

"Why? So I'll think better of you?"

She'd walked straight into that one, but that didn't make the words hurt any less. "No, I don't expect anything of the kind. Listen, I should be out on the streets, or at the police station making sure everything's okay in—"

"Everything's fine," her father interjected with a dismissive wave. "If it wasn't, don't you think Orrin would call? Talk to the boy if that's what he wants."

What the wily old fox really wanted was to eavesdrop, to see if he could get a clue as to what her plans were—as if she had an idea herself. "Don't push," she warned, then turned back to Kyle. "I'm going to change, then go into town for a while. Do I need to worry about you?"

"I won't run away again, if that's what you're asking."

"It is, and thanks."

Certain he wasn't anywhere near ready for any sign of affection from her, she excused herself and headed upstairs.

It took only a few minutes to dig a blue uniform shirt from the tote bag that Kyle had carried up for her, and to remove the patches on the sleeves. Slipping it on, she tucked the tails into her jeans.

"Your grandfather knows how to contact me," she told Kyle as she returned downstairs. Hoping he would keep his word and be here when she got back, she let herself out by the kitchen door.

No longer looking forward to reacquainting herself with the community, Taylor climbed into her father's Blazer once again and headed back toward town. Now all she felt was turmoil, which made her previous concern about being the first and only female law officer around trivial in comparison. When she came to the intersection of Main and Crooked Pine Road again, and saw a familiar old pickup surge forward to block her path, she knew she wasn't going to get any downtime to try to regroup, either.

She'd guessed he would come after her, but she was amazed to see him jump out of the still-running truck and stride to her window. "So much for any fleeting thoughts about damage control," she murmured under her breath.

"We need to talk," he said, getting straight to the point.

"I agree, but—"

"Now. Name a place or we do it here."

Taylor bit at her inner cheek to keep from responding in the same aggressive tone of voice. More calmly she replied, "Threatening a peace officer isn't exactly the way to get what you want."

"I'm not threatening a peace officer, I'm addressing the mother of my son."

Because he sounded more rational this time, she nodded. "Let's go to the station and use my father's office." Their joint arrival was bound to attract attention, but they'd already done that at the feed store. As she'd driven Kyle home, she'd spotted someone who looked like one of the Hernandez boys calling after a dog that had charged the Blazer. Since there were other businesses along that road, no doubt there had been others who'd either seen or heard a portion of their little drama being played out.

Hugh made no response to her suggestion, and only after he returned to his truck and led the way into town did Taylor know he'd accepted it. She followed, her gaze occasionally clashing with his in his rearview mirror.

As expected, several shop owners in direct view of their destination stopped whatever they were doing to gawk through windows and glass doors as they parked. Both she and Hugh ignored them, but wasted no time in entering the unlit but wonderfully cooler station.

One look at Orrin's expectant face and Taylor knew her father had phoned ahead to let him know she was coming. He wasn't, however, expecting Hugh.

"Orrin, you remember Hugh Blackstone?"

"Sure. Uh, something wrong, Miz Taylor?"

"Everything's under control," she replied, feeling less so than she had in years. "I need to use the chief's office for a few minutes. Will you hold any calls, unless there's an emergency, please?"

"Yes'm."

"And call me Taylor," she added.

"Yes'm."

Too stressed to appreciate the humorous moment, she continued on to the office. As soon as Hugh followed, she quietly shut the door. She was aware that her hand was shaking, she was shaking all over, and that was another sign of how things had changed. In the old days she would have laughed out loud at the idea of being nervous around Hugh.

"Have a seat." She gestured to the two facing the steel desk.

He remained standing.

"Okay, would you care for coffee or something else to drink? I'm sure—"

"What I would like is for the world to stop turning upside down. Or inside out. I'd settle for one."

So he wasn't as steely cool as he appeared. "I understand."

"You couldn't possibly."

"Well, of course, I don't not know what you went through in prison—"

"And you'd better pray you never do," he said, his words bearing a decided chill factor. "You also don't know what it's like to come back to the only home you've ever known and discover you have a son."

"We already covered that ground."

"You said your piece. I haven't had a chance to say mine yet."

What could he want to say except to fling more accusations at her? "I don't want to fight, Hugh. As I said, I tried to tell you, but you wouldn't see me. You wouldn't listen."

"You could have told my lawyer."

"Is that how you would have wanted to find out?"

"It would have been better than this." When she failed to respond to that, he shook his head and uttered a brief, harsh laugh. "Man, you and your old man sure did a number on me."

"He didn't know, either."

That threw him anew. For several seconds he looked as if he would challenge her on that, but ultimately he still could read her face well. "Hell. How did you manage that?"

"I left soon after you were— After the trial. Since I wasn't showing yet, people accepted my queasiness as a result of being upset over the verdict."

"They should have asked me. I could have set them straight."

"Believe what you want to believe, Hugh, but don't waste my time with the sarcasm. There isn't any name you can call me that I haven't already called myself, so just ask what you need to ask."

His strong jaw worked hard, but he accepted that. "Why did you keep him a secret from your father?"

"Because you deserved to hear first. When you made it clear that you didn't want to have anything more to do with me, I realized I had to make my own decisions. One of them was to protect my baby."

"Your father was no threat."

"No. He would have been upset—he *is* upset—but he would have come around and been there for me. I meant, I had to get away from this town. If they knew about Kyle, they wouldn't have treated any Benning much better than they did you. I couldn't ask him to pay for my mistake."

"If carrying my child was so repugnant to you, why didn't you have an abortion?"

Now he'd gone too far. Taylor slammed her hat down on the desk. She would have preferred something heavier and breakable. "I can't believe you even asked that!"

"Well? Isn't that what you meant?"

"You know damned well what I meant. God..." She turned away and pressed a hand to her forehead. When she used to imagine them having this conversation, she had always avoided considering a scenario like this. "I will not participate in this...emotional butchering. You want to hurt me? Here." She jerked her gun out of its holster and slammed it beside her hat.

The gesture had an equally profound effect on Hugh. He swore under his breath, dropped into the chair farthest from her and, leaning an elbow on one of the armrests, covered his face with his hand.

For what seemed an interminable length of time, silence reigned. Taylor didn't know what Hugh was doing because she couldn't look at him, she was too close to breaking. But she heard his heavy breathing and knew he was battling his own inner war.

"I shouldn't have said everything I did," he said at last. "I apologize."

"Accepted."

"Do you mind me asking...how did you manage? You had no education or job."

Reassured by the gruff, almost caring note in his voice, Taylor leaned back against the far wall to meet his troubled gaze. What she saw there also gave her confidence.

"I lived with Ally at first. Remember Ally Sanders from high school?"

"The rich girl who lived with her grandmother here because her parents were always traveling."

"Yes. And when her grandmother died, she moved back north to attend college. She let me share her apartment for a while."

"How long is a while? You were a kid. Now you're past thirty."

There was nothing wrong with his math. "That's really besides the point. What's more, it's none of your business, Hugh. No, don't get all uptight again. It's just that while I don't mind answering any questions you have about Kyle, my personal life is off limits."

"I'm asking, anyway."

A new knot formed in her stomach. "Kyle carries my family's name. That's all that should matter to you."

"And I think you're avoiding something. Why did you give the boy your name, besides the obvious reason, that is?"

Why bother? she asked herself. One way or another he would find out everything he wanted to know; he might as well hear it firsthand from her. "Because that's the name I took back after my divorce," she said wearily. "Satisfied?"

Hugh looked like a man who'd just taken a full blow between the eyes from a baseball bat. But after the first few moments of shock passed, he gave a brief, sardonic laugh. "You were married even before you had the baby? Hell, yeah, you were really heartbroken, weren't you?"

It was ludicrous to try to explain, but Taylor smoothed the short hair at her nape and tried, anyway. "Yes, I was on shaky ground and scared. Jim Patrick was a nice guy who I met right after arriving in Detroit, a guy studying to be a cop, and who came from a long line of cops but who really wanted to teach. He wanted to help me, and at that point I wanted help. I also thought giving my child a stable, complete home was the wise thing to do, but we'd have been better off staying friends. Just before Kyle was born Jim met someone who was right for him. I convinced him not to be dumb—about me or his career—and so he divorced me, married her and became a teacher. They have three terrific kids now."

"That's the craziest story I've ever heard."

Hugh's verbal reaction was mild compared to the disapproval, maybe even disgust, she saw reflected on his face. This was as far away from the boy and young man she'd known and loved as she could imagine him getting. If any of that person still existed, he was well hidden behind a thick armor of bitterness and resentment, and even if that armor was justified, it was difficult to deal with. She found it easier to study the laces on her jogging shoes.

"Well, they say truth is stranger than fiction," she murmured.

"Just answer me this—does Kyle call him 'Dad'?"

"Of course not." Once she'd realized the enormity of her mistake, she'd made sure she corrected things. "As I said, we remained friends, but I moved back in with Ally, struggled to finish school and took up where Jim left off as far as police training was concerned."

"You never said anything about wanting to be a law officer as a kid."

No, her whole universe had been him. Looking back she could see how that may not have been the healthiest of things. She wasn't, however, stupid enough to admit that now. "We all change, Hugh."

"And what if you'd been killed? Who would have taken care of the boy then? Emmett?"

Once again the anger and censure was there, but Taylor knew exactly how to deal with it this time. "He raised me." The challenge presented, she chose to extend an olive branch of sorts. "I think I make a good cop, Hugh. I've been well trained, and because I'm very aware that I have someone waiting at home for me, I'm very careful."

He eyed the gun as though suggesting her actions disproved her words. "So why did you quit?"

"I won't lie to you. Kyle's been getting in trouble."

"Drugs?"

"Thank heavens, no. At least I don't think so. But I knew I had to get him away from the boys he was hanging out with or else there would be that and more. I couldn't compete with that kind of peer pressure gangs present, even though we'd had a terrific relationship until this past school year. And that's it," she concluded with a shrug.

"Not quite."

This was the moment she'd always feared, and there was no escaping it as she had when she would rouse herself from nightmares. "What do you mean?"

"He's my son. He knows, and so will my mother as soon as I go back and tell her. Soon the rest of town will find out."

"Not necessarily. Neither of you needs to advertise it."

"I want him to have my name."

"What about what he wants?"

"I think he made it clear when he came looking for me."

"Curiosity isn't the same as acceptance."

"He's my son, Taylor. It will be a mistake to try to keep him from me."

"And I was your lover, but you found it easy enough to turn your back on me!" Taylor snapped. "I won't jeopardize my boy's heart—or his safety!"

Four

Even as her words slashed at him, Hugh admired Taylor's courage. Like her old man, she'd always been a straight shooter. If you didn't want to hear the truth, at least the truth according to Benning, you didn't ask. But she didn't have to remind him of how he'd treated her. That was something he'd lived with every day of his life. What she didn't, couldn't, know was that while he'd initially shut down because he'd been heartsick at what he'd seen as her betrayal, he'd also been terrified over what lay before him. The way he figured it, he'd done her a favor.

They'd been as close as two people could possibly get. Worse than death would have been to go to prison and watch their love shrivel and die inch by inch. By severing their ties swiftly and surely, he'd believed he'd been saving her—*them*—prolonged anguish. Come to find out, his stubborn silence had only added to her grief…short-lived as her subsequent marriage might suggest.

He closed his eyes and struggled to find the calm center

in this emotional storm. The past couldn't be changed, and somehow they had to get beyond its debilitating shadow. If they didn't, neither one of them would have a life of any kind left worth living.

Unused to having to deal with such a conflict of feelings, he was slow to respond. But when he did, he meant every word. "I don't want to fight with you about this."

"Do you think I do? But you're the one making demands."

He understood, he even agreed, only... "Well, damn it to hell, Taylor, what am I supposed to do when you're more independent than ever!"

"Because I've had to be. You'll also discover what triggers that independence fastest is someone dictating what is and isn't going to happen. Ask. Discuss."

Restless and frustrated, he shifted; what he really wanted to do was pace and burn off some of the energy churning within him. But this postage-stamp-size office wasn't much less confining than his cell had been.

"That's a far cry from how things worked in prison. I guess it's going to take me longer than I expected to get used to the outside world again."

Taylor didn't make any verbal response to that; however, there was no missing the body language. With her hands behind her back and her head bowed, he saw a woman who was willing to listen, but was feeling cautious. Fair enough. All he had to remember was that the Taylor he'd loved had possessed a generous heart. Maybe that girl wasn't completely gone.

"I suppose when a man finds out years too late that he's a father, he's entitled to overreact a bit."

He didn't want to feel the surge of hunger he'd experienced when he'd overreacted earlier, but it came again, strong and riveting. Hugh could only run his hands along his thighs and fight to keep his mind on the reason he'd wanted this meeting.

"So what *are* we going to do?" he asked.

"One thing I don't want to do is to make too many more decisions without Kyle's input. Even then things need to be handled carefully. Let's face it, Hugh," Taylor said, her voice growing softer in appeal, "a great deal of what happens depends on his response to you as much as how you conduct yourself under the constraints of your parole."

"In other words, now that he's had a chance to look at me, he's not sure he wants a half-breed and a convicted murderer as a father."

Despite the lack of lights, Hugh could see the effect his bluntness had on her, and her almost ill expression did cut at his conscience. Well, she was the one who'd started this "let's be honest" nonsense.

"I didn't raise Kyle to be a bigot or narrow-minded," she assured him. "And he's aware of his ethnic background, and considering all the political correctness going on these days, he found himself almost a celebrity."

"But the prison term's gonna be a problem."

"No, not the term itself, the why."

During his incarceration, as insane as it was, being known as a murderer hadn't been all bad for Hugh. It had guaranteed him some respect, fear and the much-desired space from the elements that made prisons a nightmare. He hadn't hesitated to use them all to his advantage, but out here, reality was 180 degrees different, and Taylor's announcement left him feeling the same emotions he'd felt driving into town yesterday—shame, embarrassment and humiliation. He'd known right away he couldn't spend the rest of his life burdened with those debilitating feelings, but he would be damned if he would plead for anyone's understanding.

"It's a little late for me to start arguing my case," he said to her.

"It's never too late if it means cleansing what was an impeccable reputation."

God, she was still a Pollyanna. The revelation left him unable to speak.

"Hugh…" She stepped closer. "Hugh?" Suddenly she was on her knees beside his chair gripping his arm. "Just say it once and I'll never ask it again. If not for my sake, then for Kyle's. Say it. Tell me you're innocent!"

Her touch burned him to the bone, her urgent plea seared his heart. How easy it would be to give her the answer she wanted. But what about what he wanted? Sure, the right words would prompt her to throw her arms around his neck for a few minutes, maybe even win him a night in her bed—and heaven help him, he was tempted as he'd never been tempted by anything in his life—only what would happen afterward? She'd already proved she measured love in tangibles, not faith. He could give her words, but what would he offer her when she asked for proof?

Needing space, he pushed himself from the chair and put those minimal but precious few yards between them. "I didn't play that game before," he said bitterly, "and I won't start now."

"You and your pride, Hugh Thomas Blackstone…you ask for too much!"

"And you offer too little!" He strode to the door, wanting out before she pushed him over the edge. "You have the decisions to make, not me."

Before he could open the door, Taylor was beside him, her hand covering his. "For pity's sake, don't leave it like this! You've held your silence for too long!"

Her touch, the shock of her bare skin tempting his, was too much. He closed his eyes against the raw pain and ferocious hunger that ripped through him. "I haven't been near a woman since the day they locked me up," he said between gritted teeth, every muscle hurting from his attempt to control himself. "If you have an ounce of compassion for me left in you…let go."

Instead, she tightened her fingers. "Hugh, please. I just want to understand."

"Damn you." She was killing him. Unable to stop himself, he slipped his free hand to her nape to hold her still. "Damn you," he whispered again and crushed his mouth to hers.

It hurt. God help him it hurt, but he could no more stop than he could quit breathing, because she was everything he remembered: lush, hot, generous and, even now, sweet. How could she still taste so sweet after all these years?

He groaned as she responded to him, opened to him in his greedy and desperate search for more of her. He stroked and invited, clutched her closer, wanting to absorb her like a dry, dry sponge thirsting for its native sea. His body raged and shook with fever. Thunder roared in his ears.

"Hugh. Hugh...there's someone at the door."

Not thunder after all. Someone was knocking.

As Hugh released Taylor, she spun away from him, pressing a hand to her mouth, another to her middle. He knew exactly what conflict she was feeling.

"The next time I come to you," he said, barely recognizing the thick garble that was his voice, "I want to talk to my son."

When he jerked the door open, he came face-to-face with Mel Denver. Even though it had been years since he'd seen the man who'd been one of his staunchest friends, he barely gave the local vet so much as a grim nod before brushing past him and hurrying away.

"Uh, I guess my timing leaves something to be desired."

Taylor rubbed harder on her mouth, then shifted both hands to comb back her hair. In all likelihood it was standing on end, and should be, considering the electricity that was humming inside her. "No, no. I mean, it doesn't matter. I—'' She grimaced and extended her arms. "How in the world are you, Mel?''

"Fine. Great. Couldn't wait to see you again. But listen," the flustered doctor replied, all but blushing, "I can come back later.''

"Nonsense.'' She gave her childhood friend a quick hug. "Believe it or not I'd been on my way to say hello. How's Connie?''

"I left her baking a cake for you and the family. She sends her best. Wants you to be sure to come over for a glass of tea anytime.'' He thrust her to arm's length and gave her a sheepish smile. "How do you do it? What's it been...three years since your last visit? I really did regret being so tied up the last time you were down.''

His warmth made it easy for Taylor to smile. "Right. It's your fault that too many puppies and cows and whatnot got sick.''

"Well, unlike you I look as though it's been five years since I've seen you. I wish you'd age a little and stop making the rest of us look bad.''

"Oh, stop. You're terrific as always.''

Actually, she was concerned. He did seem paler than ever, except for two spots of color on his cheeks like rouge on a doll. Of course, if his schedule was anything close to what her father usually reported when she asked after friends, that was understandable. Forever in someone's barn, or in his own offices, this modern-day patron saint of animals always seemed in need of forty winks. Right now his flaxen hair needed a cut and combing, and his pale blue eyes were mere puffy slits behind his wire-framed glasses. She hoped his pace wasn't beginning to get the best of him...or Connie. Everyone liked Mel too much to say anything to his face, but it was generally agreed that anyone who spent any amount of time around Connie Denver would start to feel as if they were being leeched of their lifeblood.

As expected, Mel dismissed her rose-colored comments

with a grimace. "Remind me to recommend a good optometrist. How's the Boy Wonder?"

"Leaping into his terrible teen years with complete enthusiasm."

"Now Emmett gets to say he told you so."

"What are you talking about?" Taylor replied with pretended indignation. "I was an angelic child."

"Well, you lived up in the stratosphere, all right. Didn't we all say Emmett would have had more luck trying to harness the wind than keeping you grounded? And our friend," he added, nodding his head in the direction Hugh had gone, "only shot you higher. Speaking of which, those were combustible emotions I sensed between you just now. Was the reunion tough?"

"I've had easier."

The vet lowered his gaze to her mouth. "Am I too late to beg you to put a bullet-proof vest over your heart?"

Embarrassed, she barely resisted touching her lips again. "Really, Mel, it's not what you think. I made him angry, that's all."

"Well, as glad as I am to see Hugh again, and as capable as I know you are, I wish he'd pick on someone his own size. You know he's apt to get the chance, too," he added, sliding his glasses back up his nose. "There's someone who's eager for the chance."

"Murdock."

"He's an on-again, off-again client," Mel said, almost apologetic, "depending on how much condescension and advice I can take."

Taylor hated for him to feel as though he needed to explain. "He doesn't deserve you, Mel."

"Well, that aside, I was out there the day he got the news that Hugh would be paroled. I'm afraid he's not going to stand for it."

This was nothing new, but Taylor didn't like hearing it confirmed. "I'm planning on going out there to talk to him."

"That should be interesting."

"It's all I can do, Mel."

"You can convince Hugh to go away the way the old dinosaur wants. Even Emmett knows it's the right thing to do."

He'd said it, true enough, but her father had a bit of the politician in him, a result of holding the same job for almost thirty-five years. "Sometimes 'wise' is misconstrued as 'right,'" she told her friend. "If the parole board thought Hugh should be returned to society, who are we to tell him that he's not allowed to come home?"

"People who want what's best for him. People who want to avoid another tragedy."

"Well, I hope they'll remember they're his friends when he tells them that he's staying. From what I've gathered so far, it wouldn't be easy for him to leave. And—"she took a deep breath "—my arrival has produced another dilemma for him."

"Jeez, Taylor." The circles on Mel's cheeks deepened. "I thought you said—"

"Not me. It's our son."

As expected, the gentle-natured vet looked stunned. Slumping against the doorjamb he mouthed, "Kyle...?"

She knew her father had kept Mel updated on her marriage and subsequent divorce right after her son's birth. She nodded to confirm what she'd kept secret for so long. "There were reasons I did what I did, but now...well, if you didn't figure it out before, you would have soon enough."

"How's Hugh taking the news?"

"Better than I deserve. But I'm not sure it's wholly sunk in yet."

That had Mel's frown deepening. "I, um, I want you to know that if you need to talk about things, if you need anything at all, you only have to holler, okay?"

Taylor stroked his arm. They'd known each other almost as long as she'd known Hugh. She'd been a witness at his wedding, if a not entirely enthusiastic one thanks to his somewhat demanding and high-strung wife. But the marriage had lasted, and she liked knowing she had a sounding board close by that wasn't her father.

"I appreciate that," she said. "Only right now I think I'd better get out to the Marsden ranch."

Making her promise once again to come out to the house soon, Mel took his leave. As soon as the front door closed behind him, Taylor hurried to the bathroom to rinse her face.

The first glimpse of her reflection had her groaning and ducking her head to the cool water. She looked...

Don't even go there.

For the first time in ages she wished she used more than long-wear mascara. Maybe some artificial color would hide the embarrassing high tone of her own skin, not to mention her kiss-swollen lips. But there was nothing she could do about the brightness in her eyes, save sticking on a pair of dark sunglasses and trying to forget how enervating, how perfect, it had felt to feel Hugh's mouth on hers again.

Her heart had yet to slow down, and butterflies were acting as if they were giddy on laughing gas in her stomach. That wouldn't do at all.

And it wouldn't do to let Hugh touch her again. Heaven knows, she'd asked for what happened, but from now, either she remembered her responsibility to Redoubt or she got out of town.

Quickly hand combing her hair, she retrieved her gun and hat, and told Orrin what was next on her agenda. Then she took off before she chickened out.

Murdock Marsden had always been a tough character to deal with and since losing Piers he'd become harder. One thing her father's calls and letters had always been full of was stories about the man's independent approach to the law. If he had the nerve to take that approach with her father, who did she think she was to make him pay attention to her? Even delighted smiles and enthusiastic waves as people on the street recognized her failed to raise her hopes. Nevertheless, that didn't mean she was exempted from trying.

The MP Ranch claimed a full third of the county's acreage. Located west and south of town, it cupped the Sangre de Cristo Mountains like a blacksmith's hand cupping a horse's hoof. They set a standard for prize beef and coveted horseflesh there that made Marsden a name to be respected throughout the southwest. Taylor had been cited by the mayor of Detroit, had met the governor, but this meeting with one of the last classical cattle barons left in the country she did not relish.

Fast closing in on seventy, Marsh remained a striking man thanks to a discipline that included plenty of physical exercise to offset a healthy appetite for the beef he raised and the wine he collected with equal zeal. A born competitor in every way, he narrowed his eyes but smiled when Taylor parked before the main house and eased from the Blazer.

"Well, well." Motioning to the cowhand who had been holding the reins on two restless horses to wait, he stepped down from the porch that ran the length of his sprawling hacienda-style home. He waited for Taylor at the base of the slate stairs, his hands on trim hips. His denim shirt was as worn as his jeans, testifying that he didn't splurge on nonessentials—at least not where clothes were concerned—and worked as hard as his employees. His silver hair curled at his nape, suggesting that he saved on haircuts, too, or else believed that, like some biblical character, his strength needed protection any way possible. "I'd heard about this, but I didn't think you'd be interested in coming back."

"I surprised myself, too." Taylor didn't smile because, unlike her father, she wasn't a politician. She didn't like Murdock Marsden, and knew he felt no serious affection toward her. At the same time, she considered herself a professional and it wasn't her intention to offend him if she didn't have to. "It looks as though you're headed out to inspect stock, Mr. Marsden, so I won't keep you."

"When the day comes that something with four legs becomes more interesting than an attractive woman, I expect to be planted, Taylor Grace. In the meantime, why don't you come up here on the veranda and I'll call Miguel to bring us something refreshing to drink."

Who said Southerners possessed all the charm? "That's kind of you, sir, but I'm afraid not today. There's a great deal to do back in town."

He didn't look pleased at being turned down, but decided against challenging her. "As you wish." He'd begun to tug off his leather gloves, but now slid them back on. He wasn't a man to ask a person anything twice, not even a woman. "What's on your mind?"

"Peace."

"Whose?"

"Everyone's."

In a face perennially tanned by the wind, Murdock's wide mouth curled downward. He could have been posing for a position on Mount Rushmore. "Meaning everyone but me. No, don't try to sugarcoat it. I'm not going to be pleased by what you're going to say, am I?"

"No, sir. But I hope you'll see the merits of my request." Taylor hated sounding as though she was a first-year law student pleading a case before a supreme court judge. Only she knew if she assumed a bolder attitude, Murdock would shut her down and throw her off his land before she got half through her speech.

He did look annoyed, but to her relief held his temper for the moment. He didn't, however, insist they sit down, and he waved away his houseman, Miguel, who Taylor saw still fit a trim white tuxedo jacket, even though his hair, like his boss's, was almost snow white.

"Get it over with," Murdock Marsden said, admiring the fine leather of his gloves.

"In short, I'd like a reassurance that you intend to obey the law."

The sun beat on them without mercy and the heat burned through Taylor with the same intensity as Marsden's eyes. Still, she held her ground. Too much weighed on her ability to do so.

"But I always obey the law, my dear."

"You've made remarks recently to suggest otherwise."

"Ah." He crossed his arms and nodded. "You've heard about my displeasure over a pollution problem in our area."

"That's uncalled for, Mr. Marsden."

"So is asking me to step back and let everything I've worked for, everything my ancestors worked for and my son died for, go to hell?"

"Mr. Marsden, your son did not die protecting the MP."

"Be very careful, Taylor," Murdock replied, his voice like cold silk. "You're fast approaching the limit of my goodwill."

"I understand. Now please understand this. Hugh Blackstone remains unharassed as long as he stays on his property and obeys the law. Are you going to have a problem with that?"

"I can tell you without contemplating the matter, girl. I want his hide. If I can't have it, I want him out of town. It's that simple."

"Not quite." Taylor had to ask. "I'm confused about this change in your attitude. You could have done what you always do, you could have gone to his parole hearing and insisted he not be let out. Why didn't you?"

There was no reading his eyes because he'd lowered them to the ground.

"Maybe I'm tired of arguing with fools."

Despite the heat, a cold dread rushed through Taylor. "Meaning?"

"You decide."

"I don't like the sound of that, Mr. Marsden."

"I don't give a flying fig, *Officer* Benning. There's a murderer loose in Redoubt. If the law won't do what they're paid to do, then I will."

"Talk like that could trigger a bloodbath," Taylor replied. "I understand that there are some in town who support you, but do you really think that would continue if they knew how deeply your logic is based on prejudice and a need for revenge?"

The tall, proud rancher didn't blink. "Well, that's for you to find out."

His blatant challenge didn't surprise her. What she would do about it, him, she would worry about later. For the moment, she needed to remind him that he didn't control everything and everyone in this county—at least not yet.

"I suppose I will," she said with a calm nod that was all bluff.

Suddenly Murdock grinned. "How's your daddy?"

The question had nothing to do with consideration and everything to do with putting her in her place. "The chief is hurting and in need of rest. He'll get it now."

"This is a big job for a little girl."

She could have kissed him for that insult. "Think so? Well, that's something for you to find out."

Her back straight, Taylor strode away and climbed into her truck. She saw Murdock studying her, his rugged but handsome face speculative. Good, she thought. She wanted to make him think twice. At the least it would buy her time. She hoped enough time to figure out how to keep this whole town from exploding wide open.

From the amount of blood rushing into his mother's face, Hugh wondered if he was about to deal with an explosion of denial or something more medically troubling.

"Are you serious?" she whispered. "Kyle Benning is your son? I have a grandson?"

"That's right." He told her about how he'd found out and why he'd run off before.

His mother pressed her hand to her mouth and one to her stomach. "I can't believe this is happening. All these years of hoping against hope that one of you..." As if she still couldn't let herself accept it, she demanded, "Are you certain he's yours?"

"Even if I didn't believe Taylor—and there's no reason she should bother lying about something that will disrupt her life more than anyone's—I'd recognize my own son."

"Hmph." His mother gave that a haughty toss of her head. "As if you're the only man on this planet with black hair and dark eyes. And you're conveniently forgetting, when it comes to deceptions, we both know what that girl is capable of."

"She didn't lie during the trial." He might have his resentments, he could still be angry about a lot of things, but Hugh couldn't let that remark stand. "She just couldn't say something under oath that she didn't have a clear answer to." Namely proof that he hadn't killed Piers. That had never been what his long silence with Taylor had been about. It was her doubt that he was, indeed, innocent that had crushed him.

"You're looking for any excuse to forgive her. Me, I don't want this. I don't want anything from her!" There was a rising panic in his mother's voice as she began wandering behind the store's front counter, fidgeting and plucking at things. "This is some kind of trick. Now that you're free, she's just trying to find someone to take care of her brat."

If anyone else had said that, they would be struggling to pick themselves up from the floor. That his mother said it hurt rather than offended, but he knew why she was fighting the news so hard. "He's no brat, Mother," he said quietly. "She's admitted he's going through some teenager stuff, but what kid doesn't? Besides, of all the people she could have announced as the father, I'm no prize."

"You are! You *are*."

He was touched by her intensity. They'd never been a demonstrative, overly emotional family, at least not since his father died. In fact, except for the passion he'd felt for Taylor, he'd always thought himself on the cool, rather remote side. His mother's outburst was unexpected, and not unappreciated.

"Your opinion wouldn't by any chance be tainted by prejudice?" he drawled, his tone affectionate.

"Ach, stop with the jokes. What I want to know is what are you going to do about this? Does the child know? How did he react?"

"He sought me out." Hugh felt a growing pride now that he'd run the scene through his mind several times. It wasn't every kid who had the nerve to face a stranger about such a thing, let alone a stranger straight out of prison. "Much more I can't tell you yet. Taylor arrived and took him home."

"She refused to let you talk to him?" His mother's outrage rose anew.

"We'll work it out, Mother." One thing he didn't need or want was her to start meddling.

"He'll come to you," she said with a decisive nod. "And if he's fair and unjudgmental, it's a quality inherited from you."

"Hmm...aren't you the woman who just called him a brat?"

She made a dismissive gesture. "I'm allowed a moment of shock. But I remember seeing him a few times over the years. He seems all right. I won't blame him for who his mother is."

"Taylor raised him in one of the toughest cities in the country. At least give her credit for that."

"If she'd been honest with us, she wouldn't have had to go there in the first place."

How easily people forgot the past—or at least edited it to shape their own perspective. Hugh sighed. "Okay. Let's let that be for now. Kyle Thomas is my son. Will you at least assure me that he'll be welcome here if he chooses to stop by and visit?''

"You have to ask? Of course, he'll be welcome! He probably needs a good meal. From the looks of that girl, she still hasn't learned how to boil water. My mother had an expression for skinny people like her—*ein Darm*. It means one intestine.''

She'd often told him how she didn't like the language of her ancestors, how she found it harsh. He also seemed to recall how she didn't get along with her mother. However, none of that kept her from using the sayings from "the old country" that her parent had taught her when it suited her.

"Mother. Stop. All the venom in the world isn't going to change what was. Besides, if the boy hears you speak of Taylor that way, you'll alienate him.''

"What kind of word is that to use with me? I don't alienate anyone…but I can't help being who I am.''

In other words stubborn and inflexible, Hugh thought without rancor. "The point is Taylor is also the law here. Like it or not, we have to respect her position.''

"Thank you for reminding me that I've lost whatever respect I once felt for Emmett Benning. The nerve of the man, bringing in his own daughter to replace him. Maybe Lew Sandoval was no good, but Emmett is crazy to offer her as an improvement. Thank goodness there's no real crime around here, or I would be afraid to leave my trailer or this store.''

Hugh hoped she was right about the lack of crime, only for a different reason. No matter what he believed when Taylor had failed him, he could not wish ill for the mother of the only child he figured he would ever have.

Bull. There's more to it. You've touched her again and that old hunger is beginning to burn a hole in your belly.

When he returned to the warehouse a few minutes later, he allowed himself an even greater honesty.

He didn't just want Taylor, he expected to have her. Whether it was a sane idea or not, he had to experience again what they'd once shared under the sun and under the moon. His was a craving and thirst born from his soul. It would complicate everything. It might even destroy him. But it was as real as the truth about his son...and Piers Marsden's murder.

Five

The next few days flew by faster than Taylor would have imagined, considering the time bombs she was dealing with in her professional and personal lives. Then again, that was the way things went with starting a new job. They'd arrived on Monday and by Friday she still hadn't gotten around to introducing and reintroducing herself to everyone in town.

People wanted to talk; they wanted news, had gossip to share. The old-timers insisted on showing her the changes in their stores or homes, dragged out photo albums of their expanding families... The newer residents needed equal if not more attention because they were skeptical of Officer Taylor Benning, as well as Taylor Grace Benning, resident and ex-girlfriend of Hugh Blackstone. Murdock Marsden had accomplished what he'd set out to do, sewing deeply his seeds of doubt about her.

That discovery made her glad she hadn't yet told him about her boy. She had no delusions about keeping Kyle's paternity a secret; already those closest to the family—Mel, Lola, a few others—knew. Many more and Murdock would either get an anonymous call or a visit from one of his supporters. She hoped that moment remained at least another day or two off; she needed every minute possible to establish herself as the lawful presence in town, as well as remind people that she was a friend.

When she wasn't making rounds through town, or keeping tabs on Kyle, she was combing through files at the station. Her father wasn't the world's most organized person, let alone a responsible administrator, but that didn't come as a new revelation. While growing up, if she'd wanted to find anything in the house, let alone know there would be clean towels or fresh bread, she had to see to those things herself. Since the station hadn't been any of her business, she'd let herself forget about it, and she regretted it now.

Her father's office remained a neatnik's worst nightmare. You couldn't tell at first, since he kept his desk relatively clear and its size made it the focal point in the small room, but everything else was crammed, stacked and basically overwhelmed with paper, and there was no organization to anything.

She spent three lunch hours just making stacks so she could process paperwork by order of importance. "Thank goodness this is a small town," she'd told her father during one of her stops at the house. "If Redoubt gets any more populated, you're in danger of being lost in an avalanche of your own neglect!"

"What neglect?" he'd scoffed. "Just because I'm not a paper pusher doesn't mean I didn't get the work done. Everything you need to know is right here."

He'd tapped at his temple. Taylor had rolled her eyes.

"That does me a lot of good, Pop. Thanks heaps. I'm going to start looking as though I have an umbilical cord growing out of my ear because I have to be on the phone with you all the time."

On Friday, however, she came upon a delightful little discovery. The rest of the station was Orrin's domain, and Orrin was quite the secretary...in his own unique kind of way. It first struck her when, early that morning, she was ready to start studying the old file on Hugh's case. Confident that she wouldn't be neglecting her other duties by doing some sleuthing on her own, she'd gone in search of the old paperwork and had come up empty-handed.

"Help you, Miz Taylor?" Orrin asked, appearing at her side.

"Uh, no thanks, Orrin," she replied, concerned that he might share that bit of information with her father. "Simply trying to get acclimated. And it's just Taylor, okay?"

"Sure."

He smiled that sweet, increasingly deceptive no-one's-home smile and shuffled back to his desk. But when a call from Sheriff Trammell sent her back to the communications room, he returned.

"Help you, Miz Taylor?"

She'd given into a helpless chuckle, partly because his "help you" sounded like "heppya," and partly because she'd had no success in getting him to be less formal. But this time because the sheriff was waiting, she'd decided to take him up on his offer.

"Well, Orrin, you'll be my hero if you can tell me where I can find paper for the danged fax machine. The copier's cabinet is locked. The supply closet is full of supplies for the bathroom, the kitchen and the cars, everything but what I need. I'm at a loss."

Without any facial change whatsoever, Orrin shuffled over to the wall-to-wall file cabinets. "Keep it under *F*," he said, pulling out a drawer marked with a bright black-and-gold sticker, the type seen on mailboxes. "See? Here it is."

The look he gave her over his sloping shoulder told her that he didn't understand why she'd had difficulty figuring that out. Taylor couldn't resist.

"Next you're going to tell me is that the copier paper is under *C*, right?"

His sweet smile grew more elfish. "Why would I do that? The copier has its own supply shelves built in under the unit. These here *C*'s are where the computer stuff's kept." He peered behind the two reams remaining. "And cassettes for the recorder, and stuff."

"I see. But the copier cabinet is locked."

He went to the *K*'s and lifted out a clear plastic fishing tackle box and pointed to the section labeled Copier. "The chief relies on me to be orderly," he said soberly.

"And so you are. I'm very impressed, Orrin."

"You need anything else, just holler."

Taylor didn't waste time on pride. "Why don't you wait a second while I refill the fax machine, and then you can give me a tour of how the rest of the place is set up."

Once alone again, she found what she had been looking for under *C/B*. *C* for closed, and *B* for Blackstone. Even though it was a depressingly thin file, Taylor eagerly carried it to her father's office. She had just begun to sort through it when the front door opened and Richard Redburn entered, owner of the local bed-and-breakfast inn, and past and present president of the chamber of commerce.

"Morning, Taylor. Can you spare a few minutes?"

She slipped the file under the desk blotter and went out into the main room. "What's up, Richard? You look...harried."

Actually, the middle-aged businessman looked like an owl that had been caught in a windstorm, thanks to the effects of today's strong breeze on his toupee. Like Mel, Richard could have been mistaken for a tourist he was so fair skinned, and the black frames of the glasses—which matched his rug—made the contrasts all the more startling. But the second-generation Redoubtian's sallow complexion was a result of his love for his business that kept him indoors seeing to the smooth running of his inn and the needs of his guests.

"I am!" he declared, tugging at the waistband of his brown polo shirt and plucking off what seemed to be a white hair. "At cats!"

"Cats?"

"Ophelia's cats. I've talked and talked to her, but she refuses to do anything about them. They're clawing the porch furniture, shedding on the cushions and turning my yard into their private litter box. I can't have it. You know photographers come from everywhere to get pictures of my flower beds. This morning...? I can bag the stuff as potpourri, there's no other word to describe the disaster. I should give it to *her*, it smells as lousy as the junk she sells!"

This kind of problem was a world away from what she had dealt with in Detroit, yet she knew she needed to address the situation somehow. "What would you like me to do, Richard?"

"Knock some sense into the woman."

"Uh-huh. Literally, I suppose, so that I get run out of town at the same time you get rid of her," she drawled.

"No!" Sighing, he smoothed his hair. "I'm sorry. I know I sound rabid myself, but you know Ophelia."

Indeed she did. The owner of Ophelia's Olla Podrida, the one-of-a-kind gift and craft shop she'd established in her lavender-and-blush home next to Richard's serene creme-and-green establishment, had always been something of a libertine. It surprised no one that she thought her animals should be no different.

"How many are there now?" When Taylor lived here as a kid, there had been at least four and as many as six at a time, large exotic specimens with fierce gemlike eyes that challenged authority with as much élan as Ophelia did herself.

"Eleven...not counting the ones that don't come out of the house."

Poor Richard. "I'll talk to her."

"Talking will do no good. We need an ordinance."

"That's your territory, not mine." He sat on the city council as well as the chamber. The police didn't make policy, they enforced the law. "But I'll remind her of what kind of health hazards her animals might be incurring, at the least an insensitivity to your patrons and her potential customers who may be allergic to felines."

Richard Redburn nodded enthusiastically. "That's it! Tell her that!" He came forward and shook her hand. "Thanks, Taylor. I knew you'd think of something."

"It's not much, and there are no guarantees, Richard."

"I just want my yard back."

Telling her to pass on his best to her father, he dashed away, exhibiting the same vigor with which he'd arrived. The door hadn't shut behind him when Taylor felt Orrin's gaze on her.

"That was very good, Miz Taylor. Miz Ophelia ain't likely to put a curse on someone who's concerned for people's allergies."

Taylor didn't know what provided more of a surprise, Orrin's analysis or Ophelia. "She's doing curses now?"

"Aw, I don't think she actually does anything serious. But Ted Posner over at the post office said he'd returned a lamp his wife had bought because it had shorted out, and Miz Ophelia told him that he must have broke it himself and that she hoped his whole house went dark. Well, don't you know not three days later his place suffered a power surge and wiped out his whole new entertainment unit, computer and everything."

Taylor had heard and seen eerier coincidences, but she also respected fate. "You've got things under control here, right?"

He looked as though she'd nominated him for congress. "You can count on me."

"Then I'll go talk to her. It's time I made a spin through the area, anyway. I'll be in touch via the radio."

"You didn't forget that the chief will be phoning to ask about lunch?"

With so much time on his hands these days, he phoned to ask if she'd taken her coffee break, or to remind her to put gas in the patrol car, which she'd taken to using these days. "Tell him that Kyle knows how to put a frozen pizza in the oven—and that I'll be there shortly after twelve. By the way, what can I pick up for you?"

After taking his order, she drove to Ophelia's, although it was a mere block away. But since she had to make rounds right afterward, and the temperature was already in the nineties, it was the sensible thing to do.

Trying to ignore Richard's supportive fist in the air as he watched from the parlor window of the inn, she entered the Easter-egg-colored house, and was immediately overwhelmed by the scent of potpourri, scented candles and cat litter. It took her a moment to adjust her eyes to the darkness of the place, which gave her an opportunity to hear Ophelia assure a customer with, "You light this a half hour before he comes in tonight and by the time you're serving dessert he won't be able to keep his hands off of you."

"Mel's not into sweets anymore."

Connie.

"It's a rhetorical statement, dear. Pour him a Scotch or brandy then, all the better. The point is he'll be putty in your hands."

Taylor stepped into the next room to see Connie Denver gnawing on her lower lip. This was only the second time she'd seen the woman since returning to Redoubt, the first to pick up the cake that Connie had to admit she'd eaten. It was a surprise to find her here of all places. When Mel had come to apologize again, he'd confided that his wife had to be coaxed to even shop for groceries these days.

"Taylor...welcome, dear. I'll be with you momentarily."

She hated that the older woman had spotted her because she'd wanted a chance to observe her friend's wife a few moments longer. "No problem," she replied, adding a friendly smile for both ladies.

Connie Denver remained as pretty as she remembered, only in a vague sort of way—like a lovely postcard that was fading from excessive light. Her once glossy brunette hair was dull and showing hints of gray, the cut blunt and the texture limp. Her once ripe figure was now probably overripe, but it was completely hidden by a washed-out peasant dress.

Taylor had wanted to call the incident with the cake her fault. She'd been a day late in picking up the cake. Now she worried that Mel was right to worry about his wife, and it wasn't just because Connie had turned into a frump.

But she was obviously trying to do something about it.

In turn, Connie stared at her like a child caught with her finger in a bowl of icing. They had never been the good friends Taylor and Mel had been, but seeing her dismay— no, dread—had Taylor wishing she'd delayed this visit another few minutes. Enough damage had already been done, and she didn't want the sensitive woman any more uncomfortable around her than she already was.

Connie abruptly turned back to the counter and stared hard at the candle Ophelia had been showing her. "I'll have to, um…"

"Think about it?" Her lips compressed, the older woman began repacking the item.

Murmuring something Taylor couldn't hear, Connie hurried out the back door, which led to additional customer parking.

As tinkling bells twice broke the speaking silence with a false cheerfulness, Ophelia shook her head, the beads in her Cleopatra hairdo echoing a more somber tune. "Don't know why I bother. She comes in two, three times a month and I never do get her to buy anything. I swear she's about as off center as the leaning tower of Pisa."

"It may be my fault," Taylor told her. "I'm afraid I remind her of too many things she'd rather forget."

Namely that Connie had been forced to testify when she'd confessed to seeing Hugh racing up the highway in the direction where ultimately Piers Marsden's body had been found.

Ophelia flicked her hand, sending the dozens of charms on her numerous silver bracelets jangling. "Don't kid yourself. She's just too much company for herself, that's all. Now you, on the other hand, are ready for the full benefit of my expertise."

Taylor glanced around at the stained-glass lamps, the exotic figurines of men and women in various intimate embraces; she could only imagine what the rest of the rooms offered. Ophelia was certainly focusing on a certain type of product these days.

"That's a very interesting statement, Ophelia, but I didn't come to shop. I came to talk about—" about to mention them, two of her furred friends inched down the stairs with regal aplomb "—cats."

"I see." The aging entrepreneur narrowed her eyes. "So a certain squeaky mouse has been whining about my beautiful babies again."

"Your *wandering* babies, Ophelia."

She considered Taylor for another long minute, then shrugged. "What the heck. I remember you as an animal lover and being fair. Let's get a drink of something cool, and you can plead his case."

Taylor didn't know if she made any lasting progress when she left Ophelia's nearly an hour later, but she didn't feel like having lunch, either. She used the cellular to phone home and inform her family, and that's when her father told her that he'd given Kyle permission to go visit his father.

"Oh, Dad..."

On Monday and Tuesday, Taylor had been hesitant about agreeing to any contact. For one thing, Kyle had suddenly had doubts, and for another she'd had Murdock

Marsden's threat on her mind. On Wednesday, Kyle vanished, only to return in two hours announcing to his grandfather that he'd visited Hugh, enjoyed a heart-to-heart and intended to go again the following day—which, regardless of her request for moderation, he did.

"You didn't say he couldn't," her father took pains to remind her.

"But he was there yesterday, almost the whole day. And the day before!"

"Three days out of thirteen years... You're right, the man's becoming a greedy sponge."

Her father's droll reply triggered Taylor's conscience faster than silence could have. All right, she thought, Hugh and Kyle deserved, needed, this time together. Her boy was becoming a man and there were conversations he should have—only not with her. Not with her father, either. According to her son, his "old man" was "butters," a two-thumbs-up rating if there ever was one. Really "phat," or was it "dope"? Both slang expressions meant "good" in teenese, but were used in completely different contexts. At any rate, Kyle had made it clear that he loved his grandfather; however, he felt the generation gap too broad at this point for certain dialogues.

Taylor wondered if Hugh understood what the boy expected of him? What if something went wrong, if something was said or taken the wrong way? If Kyle ended up disappointed in his father, or if Jane said things against her that upset the boy...

"You're jealous," her father announced, interrupting her troubled thoughts.

"I'm concerned. Hugh and Jane may recognize how smart he is, but not necessarily how sensitive. If something goes wrong over there, he could easily slip away and start hitchhiking back to Detroit before they realized he was gone!"

Her father made a dismissive sound. "You forgot one thing, baby. You're here. He's not about to leave his mama yet. That's the truth and you know it. So, admit it, Taylor Grace, you're jealous because, after all this time, you have to start sharing him.''

Was this necessary? Bad enough to have to deal with Hugh's release and his being so close, to be constantly taunted by the memories of how things used to be between them, and tempted with the hungers stirred by that kiss the other day. Now she had to listen to her father accuse her of something so immature as possessiveness.

"Are you going to be able to get your own lunch or do I send over something from Lola's?''

"Hell, don't you dare!'' Real panic echoed in his voice. "My shirts are getting so tight I'm beginning to feel like a turkey being stuffed for Thanksgiving. You take care of your own stomach, and I'll let you know when your boy gets in.''

It wasn't her stomach that needed attention, Taylor thought as she hung up, it was her nerves...and her heart. Jealousy indeed. Her feelings were more complicated than that.

She endured quite a wrestling match with herself to keep from driving over to the feed store and checking on things. But not even arbitrating the argument that followed a minor fender bender at the town's single traffic light, and spending another hour reading through Hugh's case file back at the office, helped ease her mind.

Ultimately, when she realized the typed words were replaced by nightmarish images from fourteen years ago, she snatched up her keys. "I need some air,'' she said to Orrin.

He looked at her as if picking up on her moodiness, but to her relief didn't ask where she was going and how long she would be. She didn't even know herself...until she found herself heading out of town.

She hadn't driven out of the city limits since Monday's trek to the MP, and while she didn't turn around when she realized she was on the county road that cut through Marsden land, she did flex her fingers and adjust her grip on the steering wheel. Obviously her subconscious thought this necessary, but her conscious mind was sending stress signals to her body.

Maybe seeing the place again, seeing that life, the world, had gone on will help you put closure on what happened, too.

How could she ask Murdock to let go, when she hadn't herself? Seeing Hugh again had brought that home loud and clear.

The sun was in her eyes as she reached her destination, but she left her hat and sunglasses behind as she got out of the patrol car. Heat and dust rose from the baked and rebaked ground, tickling her nostrils and throat, reminding her that she'd come out here without any water. The toe of her athletic shoe scooted away the fragile skull of a long-dead rodent. She thought it a good reminder of the wildlife and people that stubbornly stayed on here despite the elements that could so easily diminish them without prejudice or pity. She was one of those people.

She climbed to the top of the last foothill before the sharp cliffs, walked to the spot where Piers's body had been found. No evidence of that terrible day remained amid the rock and sparse vegetation, but she hadn't expected there to be anything. There was, however…something. Maybe she was imagining it, but she felt a heaviness, an aura of melancholy in the air. She'd felt it before at places where violence had occurred.

She'd turned to enjoy the view, to take a deep cleansing breath, when the hairs on the back of her neck began prickling. Something or someone was behind her, watching. Because it happened often out in nature when an animal browsing for food spotted a human and lingered to study the intruder, she didn't make any abrupt moves. Hoping it was a deer or coyote, but realizing it could also be a predator, she eased around to face whatever.

About to thumb the snap on her holster, she heard the crunch and tromp of hooves. Seconds later a horse and rider came from around a rock slide to her left. The animal snorted, and the rider swept off his hat and wiped his sweat-and-dust covered forehead.

The intruder was a predator all right. Lew Sandoval.

"If it isn't my replacement," he drawled, once again covering his close-cropped silver hair with his dusty and worn hat.

"Lew."

Big and burly, he cut an intimidating figure on a horse as he had when in a police car, and Taylor felt sorry for the horse having to carry his bulk. But Lew Sandoval could by no means be called fat. His girth was mostly muscle, and more than a few people in Redoubt had found out how painful contact with that could be. Taylor couldn't miss the considerable resentment flowing from him in waves like the heat from the ground, and decided that if he could still have this much dislike for someone he barely knew, her father had shown excellent judgment—not to mention guts—to fire the guy.

"You're on private property," he said, bringing his mount to a halt a scant yard or so away.

Taylor had no intention of being intimidated. "You don't want to take that angle."

"I'm Marsden's foreman. I have an obligation to protect his interests."

"Then you must have a great deal to do. Don't let me keep you."

He considered her for another moment, clearly intrigued by her lack of fear. "First, why don't you tell me why the law's up here?"

It wouldn't hurt to tell him the truth, although she had no doubt that it would confuse him. "If I knew the answer to that, I probably wouldn't have come. But to answer part of your question, this isn't an official visit."

His thin lips twisted into a smirk. "No? What, then? You gonna meet your boyfriend?"

"It's no secret that he ranks me in the same category that he does your boss and a number of others."

Strange yellow eyes, uncomfortably close together, didn't blink. "You don't sound happy about that. Still nursing a broken heart?"

That was none of his business, but if she said as much, it would leave only one conclusion in a mind like Lew's. "I'm tired of trying to vindicate myself," she replied, not having to work hard to express a weary tone. "He can go on with his life and I'm getting on with mine."

"So you come out here to keep company with old ghosts."

"The mountains and the sky have been here much longer than the ghosts," she said, not really expecting him to understand, nor caring.

"Yeah, well, maybe I should stick around and provide some backup. I've been seeing evidence of a big cat in the area."

Better to deal with a cougar or two than a creep like him. "Thanks, but I have to get back to town soon. This was just a brief stop."

"No need to run away on my account."

"Believe me, I'm not."

He glanced toward the Marsden ranch barely in view beyond yet another hill. "You don't like me much, do you?"

She didn't like the way things were going and wanted badly to take a step or two back from him and his horse; however, she also didn't want to give off the wrong signal. "I don't know you, Lew," she said carefully.

His gaze found hers again. "Would you like to?"

Right after they grew mushrooms on the sun. "I'm here to do a job and provide my son a good home. That keeps me fairly busy."

"In other words your old man's been telling you lies about me."

"My father doesn't lie."

His smile radiated no warmth. "You've got his blood in you all right. Same high and mighty way of talking. But I've got news for you, you keep taking up for that half-breed and you'll find out how welcome you are in that stinking town down there."

"Why are you so angry at Hugh?" she asked, honestly at a loss. "I understand how you could feel slighted by my father, but what did Hugh Blackstone ever do to you?"

"For one thing, he killed my boss's son, his only heir. You know what it's like for a proud, successful man like Mr. Marsden to have to live with that, live with the knowledge that he's the end of the line?"

Boy, Taylor thought, was he practicing making points with his boss or what? Unfortunately for him, she was the wrong audience. "No, I don't, Lew. But I do know that Piers burned a number of bridges with people in the area. He played loose with the law, took unfair advantage of his family name, and there were rumors that Noel Blackstone wasn't the only girl to have suffered his...let's call it un-wanted...attentions. If Hugh did kill Piers—and since I wasn't there, I can't say one way or another—he didn't end the life of the world's nicest human being."

"Is that the excuse you and your hypocrite father are using for letting scum like that back into town?"

A deep outrage rose within her. More than anything she wanted to make him take back his unfair characterizations, all of them. You didn't, however, provoke an unknown commodity unless you were willing to deal with the con-sequences. As it was, her silence was enough to annoy him.

"That's the way it is, then?"

Taylor watched his horse shift nervously. The chestnut gelding's eyes were too gentle for a man like Lew San-doval. "What do you want me to say? Would you like me to insult you back? What purpose would that serve?"

"I'll be sure Mr. Marsden is made aware of how things really stand," Sandoval replied, sharply wheeling the horse around. He nodded to her gun. "Next time you may not want to come up here without packing something with more kick than that peashooter. You never know when someone less friendly than me may be hanging around, eager to make points with my boss."

She'd dealt with dialogue like this before, had even handled assaults that sprang from milder situations. But considering the rifle and handgun he was carrying, this was the first time she felt at a real disadvantage. "Let's end this conversation here," she said, keeping her tone mild. "You don't want to cross any more lines of good taste, and you certainly don't want to be accused of threatening a peace officer."

He gave her an innocent look. "Threaten? Me? An ex-cop who loved his work and has only the highest regard for the law?"

Had she dismissed him as a bully? No, he was something far nastier, and Taylor didn't want to spend another moment she didn't have to in his company. But she also knew better than to turn her back to him.

"Okay, Lew. You've had your fun. Now why don't you go on with your business," she said, nodding in the direction of the ranch.

"I'd rather watch you squirm, honey."

He was going to force her to do the leaving. Accepting that she had no choice, she backed away several yards, hating having to watch his smile widen into a full grin. Only when she began the descent down the hill, did she force herself to risk turning her back to him.

His mocking laughter followed her to the patrol car.

Common sense told her that he'd merely been toying with her. She would probably be in worse trouble when Murdock Marsden learned who her son's father was, but she couldn't deny her strong relief when she had the car turned around and was driving away.

Just after turning onto the county road, she began to reach for her cellular phone. She had an urgent need to hear Kyle's voice, and she hoped he was back at the house by now. A crack, the heart-stopping knowledge of some projectile barely missing her head, followed by the almost immediate explosion of metal and glass, stopped her.

Instinctively, she ducked, tried to avoid flying debris, tried to see through a windshield that was shattering and mushrooming and tried to maintain control of the car, but the unexpected attack had her overcompensating.

The car swerved wide and two wheels dropped off the pavement, ending any hope of regaining control. Dust flew as momentum carried the vehicle sideways, broadsiding a dense thicket of scrub brush. The violence of the crash threw Taylor across the seat, only to fling her back in the next second, along with everything else loose in the car.

Her head struck something, but surprisingly she felt no pain. There was only a belated, odd thought...

Seat belt.

Six

Dazed and disorientated, Taylor wasn't prepared for the driver's door to be yanked open. Even as her mind screamed, "Gun!" she heard someone speak.

"Are you okay? Taylor! Easy, Taylor, it's me."

Mel. Relief joined with concern, and she grabbed at the front of his shirt and pulled.

"Down. Get...down."

"Hey! Did you hear me? It's Mel!"

Her tongue didn't want to form the words, her vision didn't want to clear, but her will was stronger. "Shooter. Damn it, get down!"

He did, as much from the force of her urgent tugging as her warning.

"Shooter...? Are you serious?" As anxiety replaced the concern in his voice, he craned his neck to peer at the rear window, uttered a soft epithet and immediately hunkered lower. "Do you know where he is?" he whispered, scanning the area from his disadvantaged position.

Her attempts to protect Mel had forced Taylor lower in her seat, and her ability to see their surroundings was worse than his. "Try the hill by the cliffs. Can you spot a horse and rider?"

"No. No, I don't see anyone. Who do you think he was?"

"Sandoval."

Mel gaped. "You're certain?"

"I ran into him up there not five minutes ago. It wasn't the friendliest of reunions." Taylor shifted amid the glass and litter scattered over the seat to get a better look. Considering their exposed location, they were perfect targets if someone wanted to finish them off. "He's gone. He only wanted to scare me."

"Well, I don't know about you, but I'm about ready for a new pair of pants."

The tickle of something on her cheek had Taylor lifting a hand to the spot, then higher. She stared at the red stain on her fingers. "Jeez...I'm bleeding."

"No kidding. There are several cuts, you found the worst. I don't think it's serious, though."

Because he looked more hopeful than convinced, Taylor wanted to reassure him. "You're a vet. What would you know?"

"Go ahead, have your fun," he said, continuing to look around as he reached into his pocket. "Just don't pass out on me. I'm not sure I could carry you to my truck." He took out a handkerchief and touched it to her wound.

"Thanks a lot. I'm not that big."

"Yeah, well, neither am I."

She would have chuckled if her head wasn't beginning to hurt big time. "I have to call for help."

"Good idea. You need to get to a hospital in case something's embedded in that wound."

"I don't need any hospital. I'm radioing the station to have Orrin send Jer Trammell out here."

"Reinforcements sound reassuring, too. But you may have a concussion, Taylor, and you might need stitches."

"With this thick skull? A couple of aspirins will do the trick." Telling Mel to keep down in case she'd been wrong in her guess about being out of danger, she contacted Orrin. "And you'd better let my father know," she added, knowing Sheriff Trammell was likely to call him himself.

"Why didn't you have him warn Trammell about Sandoval?" Mel asked as soon as she disconnected. "Demand he be arrested?"

"Based on what?"

Sitting up now, Taylor kept dabbing at her wound while eyeing the damage to the patrol car. There was a hole in the back window about the size of a dime. Apparently the bullet's trajectory then sent it into the rearview mirror and finally angling out the front windshield near the driver's side. It didn't take much imagination to figure out how close she'd come to tragedy.

"Based on—" Mel made an incredulous sound. "Your word as a cop, how's that? You said you saw him."

"Not aiming a gun on me." She gestured vaguely toward the exit hole. "And I doubt we'll be able to find a bullet. It would be my word against his."

"Wouldn't the gun have—what do you call it?—trace evidence, a smell that would prove he'd shot it?"

"Yes. But all he would have to say is that he'd shot at that cat he'd mentioned was in the area."

Mel nodded, his expression thoughtful. "There has been some concern about that. A few folks on the reservation lost some of their young stock." He took the handkerchief from Taylor and refolded it to a cleaner side before handing it back to her. "Having said that, I have to ask...what's Sandoval's reason for taking potshots at you? Jealousy because you got his job?"

"That offends him, no doubt about it, but I think it's primarily because he works for the Almighty Marsden."

"So you think this is about Hugh?" Mel glanced toward

the cliffs again. "Is he why you were up where Piers died?"

"Don't ask me to explain, I just felt a need to see the place again. It changed so many lives."

"Sandoval must have worried you were looking for evidence overlooked before."

"After all these years?"

"Thank goodness a client's mare needed help during a delivery. I hate to think what would have happened if I hadn't been around. Then again, maybe Hugh would have gotten here in time."

Taylor was sure she'd heard him wrong. "Say that again? What about Hugh?"

"Nothing, except that I saw him taking a load of stuff to one of the reservations earlier. I didn't know they delivered, but—"

"You're sure it was him?"

"Of course, I am." Mel frowned. "What's going on, and why do you have that look on your face? Taylor, you don't think— Not Hugh."

But the road to the reservation ran very close to where she had been, and if someone had wanted to keep an eye on her, take a shot at her, there were enough hills and scrub brush to hide them until there was ample opportunity.

"C'mon!" Mel cried, incredulous. "Hugh loved you. He would never do anything like this. For what purpose?"

Because she'd killed that love. Because she'd helped put him in prison for fourteen years. Oh, she could name several reasons for him to want to scare her witless if only to pay her back for the years he'd suffered. Or maybe like Mel had asked, he thought or *knew* there might be some evidence up there that would prove the jury had been correct in its verdict, after all.

Dear Lord, are you for real?

Her head began to throb, but it was the pain in her chest that had her closing her eyes.

"Uh-oh."

Taylor heard the rumble of a vehicle approaching at almost the same moment Mel spoke. She glanced at his profile and knew it wasn't Sheriff Trammell or any of his people. Lew?

She eased around as quickly as conditions and her body allowed her. "Oh...damn."

Hugh's truck slowed and pulled in directly beside Taylor's car. "Taylor!" he shouted, running over to her.

She didn't think she could bear to look at him. But he brushed Mel aside and took hold of her wrist, moved the handkerchief away from her forehead to see how badly she was hurt and swore.

"What happened?"

"Someone shot at her, Hugh."

Taylor forced herself to look into his face...and wanted to believe. Could a man show such shock, such dread, and be guilty of something so heinous?

"Where's Kyle?" she demanded, beginning to feel as though she might be bleeding internally. "I was told he was with you!"

"What? He was before. I guess he's home now. He wanted to come with me to make a delivery to the reservation, but you know how depressing it is out there. I didn't want him to have to be exposed to that sooner than he had to be."

"So you were alone?"

Mel stepped forward. "Taylor, don't do this."

Hugh looked from her to Mel and back again. His confusion was as real as his concern for her. She saw it then as clearly as she had ever seen anything, and could have wept with relief.

"Would someone please tell me what's going on?" he demanded. "First you tell me that someone shot at you, and then you ask me—"

The fates weren't going to be kind, and he was too sharp. She saw realization light a fire in his dark eyes, watched his body grow very taut.

"You can think that of me?" he said so softly only she could hear.

"No."

"Don't lie. I can see that you do."

"For a moment. Only——"

"Send Mel to the truck, then," he interjected. He shot their friend a brief glance. "Look for a gun. Go on. Go find out if I'd be willing to break my parole just when I've found something to live for again."

The very idea when put into words made her feel more of a fool than she'd been calling herself. But the damage was done. "I'm sorry. But I had to consider every angle."

"Is that so? Did you accuse him, too?" he asked, nodding toward Mel.

"Hugh...please."

"Save it. I've heard more than enough." His bearing rigid, his expression closed, he considered the car. He looked about ready to explode. Rising, he scanned the area. His gaze lingered at the point by the cliffs, then he snapped at Mel, "Have you checked out the area?"

"Are you serious? With what as my protection? A hypodermic needle?"

"Jer Trammell's on his way." Taylor didn't want Hugh to take out his anger on Mel. "Besides, Lew Sandoval has to be back at the MP by now."

"What's he got to do with any of this?"

At least her mention of the ex-cop had gotten Hugh to look at her again. Briefly, Taylor filled him in on their confrontation, but she had mixed emotions about having shared the information.

"Are you sure you didn't get that injury to your head before the accident," he said, furious, "because you're showing an uncommon lack of sense even for you. You shouldn't have been up there alone, Taylor."

"Look, I'm fine. It's over and——"

"Is it? It doesn't sound like that to me. It sounds as though you've stirred a real hornet's nest with someone, and you're sitting out here inviting Sandoval or whomever to go for round two! Where the hell is Trammell?''

He was yelling by now and Taylor held her other hand to her temple as the sound effects played darts through her brain. ''It's only been minutes. I'm sure he'll get here as soon as possible.''

''Well, that's not good enough. I've got rope in the truck. I'm going to pull you out and get you out of there.''

Without waiting for any other arguments he strode away. Mel gave her a sympathetic, what-did-you-expect look and followed to help.

Over the next several minutes, the two of them maneuvered vehicles and attached the rope from Hugh's truck's rear bumper to her car's front one. Then Hugh pulled the patrol car out of the soft shoulder and back onto the pavement.

He determined that the tires were still road worthy, if out of balance. ''But with that windshield, you can't make it on your own. Can you manage to keep the car semistraight while I tow you?''

She didn't want a tow. Unfortunately, no other help had yet to arrive and she was feeling sicker by the minute. What's more, Mel had made it clear that he wasn't about to challenge Hugh. Of course, she couldn't blame him for that; Mel wasn't a fighter, and even if he had been, he was at a physical disadvantage to someone like Hugh.

With the sparest of nods, she thanked her friend for his timely arrival and let Hugh take control.

Close to town, Mel veered off on his road, while she and Hugh had to deal with a good number of gawkers once they got to town. Even more people stepped out of stores to stand on the sidewalks when she parked her car and climbed into Hugh's truck. Oddly enough, those stares were nothing compared to dealing with his silence on the trip to her father's place.

Once at the house, she decided they couldn't part without her trying to ease some of the tension between them. However, finding the right words remained the problem.

"I know you're upset with me," she began as he pulled into their driveway, "and maybe you have a right to be. But I would never be able to convince myself that you wanted to hurt me. Not really."

"Right. That's exactly what you were ready to accept."

"No! I just... I have to put everyone through the same litmus test, Hugh. Call it a reflex from being a cop for so long, and being raised by one for even longer. I can't explain it."

One sidelong look from him told her that he didn't want her explanations or excuses, his opinion held. Crushed, Taylor was grateful to see Kyle race from the house, and her father on crutches at the front door. Apparently the news had scared the heck out of her men, and for once she didn't mind the idea of being fussed over a bit.

"Jeez...you look bad, Mom," Kyle said upon opening her door for her.

For him she managed a wry twist of her lips. It was the closest thing she could get to a smile. "Yeah, but you should see the other guy." No matter what, she didn't want him picking up on the tension between her and Hugh. But the boy didn't so much as look at his father—and Hugh hadn't turned off the motor of his truck.

"What am I missing here?" she asked, looking from one of them to the other.

"Ask him."

Kyle's curt response bordered on the rude, but through her now-pounding headache, she picked up that he was hurting. Something had happened between father and son, and it hadn't been good.

"This isn't the time," Hugh said to him. Neither his tone, nor his expression, left room for compromise. "Help your mother inside and see that she gets to a doctor."

"I don't need you to tell me how to take care of my mother."

The turnaround to his behavior made Taylor dizzier than ever. "Kyle! Go to your grandfather. I'll be right there."

"I think you should come now."

Just what she needed, a power play. She reached through the window and covered her son's hand with her own. "I'll be right there," she said more gently.

The boy stormed off. It wasn't the first time he'd done that, but Taylor knew this time was different. She turned to Hugh, intending to find out what had happened so she could try to repair whatever damage was done.

"I knew this wouldn't be easy, but I had no idea it would be this hard, either," she said to him.

"It's no big deal, and I told you about it before. He wanted to go to the reservation with me. I said no, and he got puffed. If he wants to act like a brat, that's his decision, but he won't do it around me."

While Taylor would readily admit that Kyle had his moments, such labeling wasn't fair. "He just needs some time to get adjusted to the idea of having a father," she replied. "The same way that you need to get used to the fact that you have a son."

"I'm there, believe me."

"A *teenage* son."

That had him pausing, considering...and finally slumping back in his seat. "This is so damned hard."

"The good news is that it's a lifelong struggle."

That earned her a droll look. Then his gaze slid to her forehead and he drew a deep breath. "Go get that head taken care of. If you're right, there'll be time to tear each other up over the rest later—and to get yourself shot at."

Taylor refused to take offense, she'd seen his eyes when he'd first thought her seriously hurt. Easing out of the truck, she said through the window, "You be careful, too. Trouble is coming."

"Then take off that badge and get Kyle out of here."

She didn't reply because she couldn't say anything he

would want to hear, and as expected, Hugh ground the gears as he put the truck into reverse and pulled away.

"Want me to throw you the keys to my truck so you can go after him and write him a citation?" her father said as she joined him on the porch.

"You're turning into a true comedian, Dad."

To her amazement, he slipped an arm around her shoulders and kissed an unbruised part of her forehead. "Merely trying to get your mind off your other problems. You look like you went through a meat grinder, honey."

She felt it, but she was darned if she would admit it to the old warhorse any more than she did to Hugh. Knowing him, he would start showing up at the station and that would set back his recovery schedule all the more.

Coaxing him back inside, she replied, "I'd look better by now if your pal Trammell would have shown up."

"He phoned Orrin when you were dropping off the car at the station. Orrin spotted you and let me know. Anyway, Jer said two of his people had been waylaid on a wild-goose chase—clearly a crank call—and he'd been in a meeting with an assistant state attorney general."

"I guess I would have had the mother of all floral arrangements from the sheriff's department if whoever shot at me had been more successful."

Her father eased himself onto the couch. "I'm no happier about this than you are, Gracie, but we're not going to get to the bottom of this by being sarcastic." He nodded toward the stairs. "I told Jer that it looked as though you were okay, but that we would need to meet with him about the incident. He'll be here in a couple of hours. Do you want to go clean up and take a minute to talk to the boy? Do you need Doc Davis to slip you in at his office? A call is all it would take to walk in. Say the word."

Taylor paused before a mirror in the hallway and wanted to turn the thing around. Even she had to admit she looked terrible; however, when she considered how bad things could have gone, she could go on. Very easily.

"Poor Orrin's probably being bombarded with gossip mongers," she told her father, not quite entering the living room. "I'll go clean up, fill you in and then get back to town. It's important the town be reassured right now."

Her father's eyes grew overbright. "You are— Have I told you lately how proud I am of you?"

"You showed me, Pop," she replied softly. "You gave me a job. And I promise you, I'll be damned if Redoubt is going to slip back a hundred years to its gunslinger beginnings."

Twenty minutes later, much refreshed if not at peace, she returned downstairs to find her father had poured her a glass of iced tea. She saw the spoon in the glass and lifted an eyebrow, suspicious.

"Yes, it has sugar in it," he replied, his tone challenging. "I'll bet you a week's pay you skipped lunch, and after all the adrenaline you burned, you need something to keep you going."

"Nag, nag, nag," she murmured. But she stirred the crystals that had sunk unmelted to the bottom of the glass and sipped obediently.

"And how are things upstairs?"

"I knocked. He said, 'Leave me alone, please.'"

"Sorry to hear that."

"Not me. 'Please' is a good sign. 'Please' is terrific. He simply thought this was going to be a piece-of-cake job for me, and dullsville for him. To discover he has a father like Hugh, and then seeing me like this," she said, then gesturing to her bandaged forehead and the other web-fine scratches, "well, he just needs what we call sorting and sifting time. The 'please' is my little boy saying so far, so good."

"You're the boss. So about what happened today— aside from what you told Orrin—you don't have to justify going out there. I understand the place holds a huge history for you, but the risks, Taylor."

"You're right, you're right. I should have known Sandoval would show up.'' She quickly filled him in on what that dialogue had been like.

''Son of a snake charmer— All the years I tried to work with that guy...''

''Forget it, Dad. He showed up at a time when you needed help and he had the credentials.'' Her father had always been fair to generous when it came to supporting the people around him. Orrin Lint was a good example. The flip side was that people like Lew Sandoval slipped through the filter of his too-generous heart. ''So you agree that it was probably Lew Sandoval?'' Taylor asked, wanting to make sure she understood him.

''He was there, he had a motive, and you said you saw the rifle on his saddle.''

''Do you think he meant to kill me? He could have— me, Mel, all of us. Why didn't he?''

''It's not his intent to kill, only to intimidate on behalf of his boss.''

''And what if you're wrong? What if he's doing this because he's the one who really killed Piers?''

Her father whistled silently. ''Oh, baby. Be careful.''

She expected this reaction and nodded to reassure him. ''Believe me, I am. But you should know I've dug out the old case file.''

''You've really changed your mind about Hugh being guilty? Just like that?''

''I can't explain it. But when he arrived at the scene and saw me...'' She closed her eyes afraid she would blow it. Clearing her throat she tried again. ''I don't think he meant for me to see it. Maybe he didn't even realize what he was exposing, but I saw...and I know.''

''For your sake, I hope you're right, Gracie.''

''I am. And you know what? That makes me terrified for him.''

''You'll be on your own for dinner.''

Hugh inclined his head as his mother searched for one

excuse after another. What did he care about food? Not only didn't he have an appetite, he didn't want to explain why he wasn't hungry. For the moment, though, his whole concentration needed to be on Noel, who had phoned during his absence. She had asked their mother to fly out to Arizona, but hadn't explained why beyond admitting to some personal problem. Since Noel had been living a life as chaste as his—maybe more so—that had been enough to convince him to do what needed to be done and get his mother on the next flight out there.

"I can get you to Albuquerque in two hours," he said after she'd passed on all the information she'd had. "Plenty of time to make that flight you called about. I think you need to go."

"She might be overreacting," his mother replied. "Maybe she only needs to talk. We can do that by phone. What if I arrive and everything's resolved?"

"Then you'll have a nice visit, which is long overdue, anyway." Hugh had never seen her so fidgety. Usually strong and pragmatic, she prided herself on a common-sense approach to everything. That his sister had reached out and admitted to having "man troubles" shouldn't have rattled his mother so...except that Noel hadn't let anyone from the opposite sex get within a block of her since Piers Marsden had gotten his hands on her. "The point is you and I both know that she's not overreacting," Hugh continued. "She would never ask if she didn't really need help. What's more, I'm perfectly capable of holding the fort here for a few days."

"I wasn't suggesting you wouldn't!"

"Then it's settled."

That had his mother looking more torn than ever. "Don't push. You don't think I've heard about what happened today? When were you going to tell me, after I phoned to let you know I'd arrived at Noel's apartment?"

"There's nothing to tell. Taylor had an accident, but she's all right."

"Someone shot at her! Someone said *you* did it!"

"They were wrong," he said matter-of-factly, although he seethed at the gossip. Who the hell had started the rumor? Surely not—

"Someone else said that you were the one to bring her home and that you two acted like you were the only people in town."

"If I'd left her out in the middle of nowhere to bake, no one would have anything to talk about!"

His mother crossed her arms. "That's not the denial I'm waiting for."

Exasperated, Hugh crossed to the bedroom closet of her little trailer, dug for her tote bag and handed it to her. "Pack. I'm going out front to lock the warehouse doors, and in case we're overrun with business while I'm gone, I'll put up a sign explaining we're closed until tomorrow. I'll be waiting for you at the truck."

"That woman will tie you in knots just as she always did," his mother called after him.

He refused to be baited. "Are you going to call the airlines and confirm that reservation or am I?"

In the end she went. On the drive to the city she spoke of the old days, to excess, a sure sign to the degree of her nervousness. Those memories of picnics and school projects, the yearly trip to the state fair that had been a tradition for the family. They stirred bittersweet memories he could have done without under the circumstances. But he knew it was his mother's way of coping. She desensitized herself to yesterday's grief and today's worries by reliving those moments when life was good to them. It wasn't her fault that his male psyche didn't work in the same way.

By the time he was watching her plane rise into the orange sky, he felt as though a car window had shattered around him. Yes, he hoped Noel was all right; he had even reminded his mother three times to be sure to let him know what was up as soon as she learned anything. But he was glad to be alone at last.

He made the drive home appreciative of the silence. Lost in his own thoughts, he didn't miss turning on the radio, which used to be a habit when he was younger. Traffic was light and the weather clear, and the old truck, rattles and all, covered the miles home fast enough. Even so it was dark when he returned to Redoubt.

The last thing he wanted to see as he pulled up to the store was Emmett's Blazer parked there. For a moment he simply sat there after he killed the truck's engine, not sure he was up to this. Her.

He climbed out of the truck, and she did the same. He went straight to the warehouse door; she followed.

"I saw the note," she said in lieu of a greeting. "What happened?"

He pulled it off and crushed it between his hands, mostly to avoid looking at her. He didn't ask how she was feeling—if there were stitches beneath that bandage on her left temple, if she'd suffered a concussion. He wasn't going to care. He *wasn't*.

"Don't you have anything more important to do?" he muttered, about as friendly as Tito's dog snarling behind its fenced pen across the street.

"Not at the moment. What's the family emergency? Is your mother all right?"

"She's fine. It's Noel."

Hell, what resistance.

"Oh, no! What's happened?"

He sighed in frustration at his inability to locate the proper key on the ring. "I don't know. We got a call and my mother flew out to be with her. I'm supposed to hear from her later. That's all I know."

"Do you want company while you wait?"

He couldn't get the door unlocked fast enough. "No."

And don't you dare add "thank you." It'll just encourage her.

She didn't need encouragement, she was as determined as the rottweiler now chewing on the chain-link fence. "I don't mind. I won't be able to rest anyway, not until I know she's okay."

He'd stepped inside, and glanced back to tell her it wasn't going to happen—only she wasn't there. He made a complete turn and discovered she'd snuck in behind him.

"Taylor...this isn't a good idea. In other words, I don't want you here."

He thought being blunt, almost rude, would do the trick. He wasn't, however, prepared to see, despite the limited lighting, such anguish in her eyes.

"Please don't shut me out."

He'd begun to walk away, his intent to get to the little office that doubled as his bedroom, his sanctuary, his cell; but hearing her plea, he swung around and grabbed her, gripping hard to keep from shaking her silly.

"Don't you understand? Can't you figure out that I can't do this, be around you without...without..."

She laid a hand against his cheek. "It's all right, Hugh. I'm hurting, too."

Seven

He'd tried to warn her, would have protected them both from this if he could, but she wouldn't listen, and her touch set off a chain reaction in him like a dam finally bursting under too much pressure. Up rose a sea of long-suppressed needs that literally forced the breath from his lungs. Desperate, Hugh clasped one hand behind Taylor's head and sought her mouth with his like a suffocating man seeking an elusive stream of sweet air.

That first kiss earlier in the week had been meant as a punishment, and this one a theft, but once again she failed to respond the way he'd convinced himself he wanted, forcing the admission that he'd been lying to himself. What he wanted, craved, was this—the unhesitating yielding, the generous offering, the wild eagerness of her own mouth and hands.

He pressed closer to her softness and rising heat, and urged her on. Within moments, even though they were already breathing hard, it became apparent that kisses and caresses weren't going to be enough. When his hands tangled with hers at her gun belt, he knew she agreed.

The only light came from a neon sign advertising a soft drink company long out of business. It bathed them in a surreal blue that made the dots of perspiration appearing on her smooth forehead seem more like a fine dusting of precious gems. Before they were through, he vowed, her whole body would look dipped in the stuff. It wouldn't be difficult—their only source of fresh air came from the big wall fan across the warehouse that sucked out what heat it could from the stifling metal building; there was nothing to relieve the new heat that their growing passion generated.

Taylor finally succeeded in removing her belt and gun, and blindly sought a safe place to set it. Hugh corrected her aim, initiating a dull clatter as it landed on an empty display rack. Then, without breaking the kiss, he backed her to the door, where he turned the dead bolt.

"We're not going to make it to the bed," he said, pinning her against the steel with his lower body. Their fit was more perfect than he'd remembered in his dreams, and answering to the pull of the most irresistible magnet force, he strained to get closer yet.

"Who cares?" she whispered back into his mouth.

Yes, this is what he'd been living for, why he'd survived all he had. The reason he had a pulse, why he bothered to breathe at all, was to reexperience this—their indifference to surroundings, to time, their mutual agreement that if they didn't merge again, and soon, they might fragment, explode. Consequently, as she tore at the buttons on his shirt, he was releasing hers. Out of the corner of his eye he saw a thigh-high pallet of fifty-pound sacks of shell corn. It would have to do.

One step, a dancelike quarter turn, and he had her there, only to have to deal with more intense sensations as she drew his hard, aching body over hers. Necessity then became a driving force. Movements grew frantic; belts and zippers were tugged, and pushed aside; clothes were flung open or shoved down; and none too soon feverish skin met feverish skin.

"I need..." he whispered, his voice becoming a raw plea as she closed her hand around him. "I need...I need you..." And then he sucked in a sharp breath as she brought him to the searing, moist heat he'd believed he would never know again. Groaning, he surged forward, and reunited himself with his sanity.

As Taylor gasped and drew him closer, his stomach-twisting pleasure sharpened, shaving the thin line between ecstasy and agony. He closed his eyes tight, felt his heart swell, his blood pound and every vein in his body strain to contain it all. He was so close...he didn't dare move. But it had been too long, too long, and joy wouldn't allow him to stay still, either.

"It's all right."

Taylor's whisper stroked him from the inside out, and the kisses she rained on his face, neck and shoulders cut through the last threads of his control. Fastening his mouth to hers, he surged into her arching body, felt her trembling around him and lost himself to the most powerful climax of his life.

For a disconcerting length of time afterward he couldn't catch his breath, but he wasn't the only one; Taylor was caught up in her own moment. It had been a long time since he'd experienced anything like this, and he was feeling extremely naked in the emotional sense.

His heart pounding mercilessly, he tried to ease up onto his elbows. Better to put some distance between them before she discovered how this one brief taste of her didn't begin to sate a starving body and soul.

Taylor tightened her arms, stopping him. "Not yet."

"This is a lousy bed. Your back—"

"Do you think that matters? I thought I'd never feel you inside me again. Nothing else matters."

His body pulsated with new life, obliterating any further

chance of denial, but he'd been kidding himself to even try. This was the woman who had consumed his thoughts for virtually every waking hour of the past fourteen years, and most of those when he'd slept. What else could a man ask for except that his beliefs and desires be echoed by her? At the same time, old hurts clung stubbornly.

"Nothing?" he heard himself ask as, ready or not, his world slipped back into sharp focus. "Those are kind words for a murderer."

To his amazement she neither flinched or protested.

"That's not going to work, Hugh."

"No?"

"Uh-uh. The tough guy approach has run its course— at least with me."

"Is that so? Why?"

"Because I know now. You slipped this afternoon, just for a moment, but that was long enough. I finally saw the truth."

She smoothed back the hair that had fallen onto his forehead, stroked the tense plains of his face, and Hugh thought he had never seen such a beatific expression. Her face virtually glowed.

His throat tightening, he asked, "Which is?"

"You didn't do it. You didn't kill Piers."

"Is that how you were able to give yourself to me? You convinced yourself that you were having sex with an innocent man?"

"It wasn't merely sex," she said softly.

He wanted to argue the point, but how could he when his body was announcing that he wanted her again? Beginning to feel a little desperate, he muttered, "Call it what you want. The problem is we took a stupid risk by not using anything."

"Worried that I'll get pregnant and slap you with a paternity suit? Something tells me, with my track record, a judge would throw the case out of court for wasting his time on the obvious."

"Don't joke about it!"

"Why not? You're trying to hide that you still care, that you're glad I know the truth now."

"Would you please drop it!"

Her eyes searched his face. "All right. What do you want to talk about if the past is off limits? Your family is, too, and so are our feelings. Our son? By the time I give you a comprehensive profile about him, he'll have changed into an entirely different human being. Teenagers make the terrible twos seem like a party.

"I know," she continued, tightening her inner muscles around him. "Why don't we skip conversation altogether."

"Taylor..."

"Have sex with me, instead." Her hands moved like spirits over his chest, soothing, provoking. Her smooth thighs caressed his hips. "Do you like me calling it that? You must. I can feel you...you're so hard again."

His skin felt singed wherever she touched him, and inside...inside the hunger was growing worse than before. "What are you trying to prove?" he growled, torn between wanting her and wanting to hate her for having this power over him.

"That I'm not going to be so easy to push away this time. That to be with you, I'll do anything you want, be anyone you want. Just make love with me, Hugh," she whispered, drawing him closer and closer, until her breath teased his lips. "We never hurt each other this way."

As the tip of her tongue darted across his lower lip and teased his tongue, he knew she'd won. He could no more deny himself this, her, than he could will his heart to stop pounding in his ears.

"Just not here," he replied hoarsely.

"Where, then?"

"I'll show you."

As beds went, the cot Hugh had carried her to was dreadful, but since it was all that was available to them short of venturing out back to his mother's trailer—Taylor barely managed a shudder at the thought of having ended up there—at least it provided a somewhat softer cushion. But good grief, it was hot. Even though they were completely naked now, the warehouse office was almost as small as her father's. With only the one door for ventilation, they were practically panting like puppies that had run too hard for too long. Of course, what they'd just done had been equally demanding.

Finally rousing, Hugh swore breathlessly and eased to her right side. "I'm crushing you."

"You can't crush liquid and I think that's what I've been reduced to."

He pulled at a corner of the top sheet mangled beneath her to blot her damp skin. "I'm sorry. Keeping physically fit in prison is as much a way to kill time as it is some deterrent to harassment. But the downside is that muscle density has made me heavier."

She couldn't believe he was apologizing for that. "You're a beautiful man, Hugh. I'm not complaining about anything but the heat. Sweat on a woman isn't exactly considered a sexy feature."

"It works on you."

"Yeah, right."

Hugh tossed the sheet aside and reached behind him to push the button on his desk lamp. The romantic blue glow was abruptly replaced by stark fluorescent reality.

About to groan in despair and protest, Taylor saw Hugh's intense expression as he studied her body, and like a blind man using braille, "reading" her with his hands from head to ankle.

"It works on you," he said again, his voice more gruff this time. He added a tender kiss to her left breast, and the feel of his lips as well as his returning arousal thrusting against her thigh had a soft whimper locking in her throat. "You're not human."

"Human enough. Just deprived for too long."

With that he opened his mouth over her breast, wetting her and sucking until, with a gasp, Taylor drove her hands into his hair and forced his mouth up to hers. Their lips clung, their tongues teased and tormented, until soon—as had always been the case between them—the most innocent, tender kiss grew into a near compulsion to get into each other's skin.

This time it was Hugh who uttered a desperate sound and, tearing away, pressed his face against her belly. "Of course," he said, thickly continuing his explanation, "having my first and only lover naked against me is a powerful turn-on, too."

First and only. The admission brought an unexpected pain that had Taylor shutting her eyes tight. She knew he didn't mean to say that as an intentional slap—or did he? In any case, the reality of their situation was that they'd both made decisions that had completely altered their lives.

"Bad timing," Hugh muttered. When she failed to respond, he sat up to look at her.

"I wondered if that would upset you."

White-hot heat burned in his eyes. "Hell, yes, it upsets me!" Swearing, he swung his feet to the floor. With his back to her, he said more quietly, "There were nights when I would lie in my cell ready to bash my head into the metal bars to stop thinking about what you might be doing, and with whom."

Taylor reached for him, but drew back when he stiffened. "Hugh...it may not make any difference to you, but Jim was the only one there was."

"Oh, jeez. Do you think I was asking?"

"You have a right to know. He's a sweet man, a good man—"

"Taylor, you'd better stop there."

"But I couldn't fall in love with him," she said, ignoring his warning because she needed to get the words out. "It wasn't very good between us."

"Taylor!"

"We were lucky to be able to part as friends, considering what a failure we were as lov—"

Before she could finish, Hugh swung around and closed his hand around her throat.

"Stop! Don't you get it? It happened! You were mine and it happened."

But only because she'd believed he hated her, that she would never see him again. As a result, she'd turned all her thoughts, her energy, to the child she'd been carrying, determined to give him as normal a life as possible. Too late she'd realized that Hugh would come between her and any man she came in contact with. It seemed her one mistake would stand between them forever.

Heartsick, she brushed his hand away and began rising herself. Before she could succeed, though, Hugh snaked a hand around her waist and dragged her back against him.

"Wait."

"Let go, Hugh. You needn't say more, and you certainly can't call me anything worse than what I've called myself."

"But I can't let you go, either," he said, pressing his face into the curve of her neck and shoulder. His arm, a veritable metal band around her waist, physically proved his words. "This afternoon when I saw how close that bullet came to you, I nearly lost it. Then seeing the doubt in your eyes when you looked at me..."

"For an instant!" she cried. "For an instant! And ever since, I wasn't afraid *of* you, Hugh, I was afraid *for* you! For what that shooting had to mean."

He pressed his whisker-rough cheek against hers. "That's the worst of it. I'm free, but instead of anything being resolved, the insanity is starting all over again, and there's no one to try to stop it but you—the mother of my son!"

Taylor was about to respond to that when the phone rang. She expected Hugh to release her and to reach for the phone on the desk; however, by the fourth ring, it was obvious that he had no intention of doing so.

"That has to be your mother," she said, gazing at the far wall that was barren except for a calendar advertising ranch supplies.

"She'll call back."

"She'll be upset. She knows how long it takes to get back from Albuquerque."

"Yeah, but if I answer right now, she would hear too much in my voice."

That was both the sweetest and saddest thing he could have said. "You don't want her to know about us."

"I'd prefer no one know about us, but I realize that's not possible the way gossip spreads in this town. Mother even knew about me driving you home before I could tell her. Taylor—" he turned her to face him "—do you realize the ramifications of that? Hasn't it struck you that, besides my problem with Marsden wanting my head on one of his fence posts like some varmint trophy, the murderer is out there, too? The thought's been driving me nuts for years, and now considering what you dealt with today, I think maybe he's warning you not to get any ideas about starting up another investigation."

"I posed that idea to my father," Taylor said, nodding. "That maybe Lew Sandoval is more than Murdock's hired gun, so to speak. What if he took the job to make himself look less like a suspect?"

"Sandoval...but what would've been his motive for killing Piers?"

Taylor grimaced. "That's what Sheriff Trammell asked. My father doesn't reject the idea completely, but says that Lew knew not to mess with Murdock's son the way he did with others in town. He doubted they had much contact. I guess I'm back to studying the case file that I finally dug up this morning," she said, concluding with a shrug.

Hugh got a strange look on his face.

"What?"

"This morning? You said 'finally this morning.'" His look was piercing. "Blue. You've been fighting to keep the faith all along?"

His husky voice, as well as the emotion in his eyes and his use of his nickname for her, compelled Taylor to lean forward and gently kiss him. "With no help from you, Blackstone."

He swept her against him and back onto the cot. Just as his mouth covered hers, they heard a beeping sound. Taylor groaned.

"My beeper. Where are my jeans? Damn, look at the time," she said, checking her watch for the first time since her arrival. "That's my father, or Kyle. They probably tried to reach me on the cellular and Orrin by radio, and are having a group fit. I have to go."

"I did figure that out."

She paused in the midst of hooking her bra. He lay sprawled across the cot watching her, so gorgeous, so dear, she launched herself across the few feet separating them and threw her arms around his neck. Yes, she had to go, but not without that kiss that had been interrupted.

"Thank you for this," she murmured when she could speak again. "This is the sweetest moment in my life since Kyle was born."

Hugh didn't look convinced as he eyed the room. "It shouldn't have happened here. This place isn't much better than my cell. Good enough for me, but—"

"I'd have come to you there—anywhere, if you'd have let me."

His hold tightened and she felt his heart beat fiercely against hers. "Don't say things like that to me, when I have to behave." He did, however, kiss her again as she attempted to finish buttoning her shirt.

It took her another minute to make it into the warehouse. Shoes, belt, holster, gun...she got herself put back together. When she looked up, she found Hugh leaning against the doorjamb and he had yet to put a stitch on.

"Don't you dare follow me outside. As it is, I'll be lucky if some nosey biddy isn't out there with their video camera. Will you let me know about Noel?"

"Will you take care of yourself out there?"

"Of course."

"Taylor, about that case file...does anyone besides your father know you're studying it again?"

"Jer Trammell. Well...and probably Orrin. It's in the office and he has access."

"Watch your back."

She couldn't believe he'd said that. "Orrin? He's a sweet, harmless little guy who worships my father. Besides, he wasn't even at the station back then. Not even in Redoubt."

"Where was he?"

"I don't know. Around the county doing odd jobs." Seeing his eyebrow lift, she sighed. "Not Orrin, Hugh."

"Okay. Sorry for sounding desperate."

"You have every right to," she said softly. "And I am going to help you get this resolved. You'll have your reputation back. People will beg to call you their friend!"

"The only begging I want to hear is yours...for me."

Taylor wanted badly to yield to the invitation in his eyes, close the small distance between them and spend the rest of the night giving him what he wanted, what she wanted, too. But she had responsibilities and had made commitments.

"Soon."

"Deal."

"Later, Blackstone."

She had her hand on the door when he tugged her back and into his arms for one last devastating kiss.

"Or sooner, Blue. Try for sooner."

Taylor did get to see Hugh over the next few days, but glimpses and a stolen five minutes here and there were about the sum of it. The job her father said would be an exercise in seat warming had her going virtually from early morning until evening. Due to the shooting incident, store-owners wanted assurances that Redoubt wasn't turning into the crime capital of the state. The city council requested a formal report and meeting to review the additional expense for repairs of the patrol car. Tito Hernandez's rottweiler escaped his pen, and suddenly one of Ophelia's cats was missing. Traffic control was provided for two funerals, and the senior citizens who met for bingo at the civic hall re-quested her presence on Tuesday and Friday nights, fearing a robbery now that "undesirables" walked the streets of their town. In the hours in between, she worked at the station.

She tried to be home every night for dinner and spend what was left of the evening with Kyle. Because there hadn't yet been time to drive to Albuquerque to buy the computer she'd promised him, most of their communica-tion time was spent shooting baskets as her father used to do with her and Hugh years ago. A suggestion to invite Hugh to join them was rejected, Kyle making it clear he had no interest yet to give his newly discovered parent a second chance at earning his affections.

It was ten days after their arrival, the morning following a very stressful Fourth of July, thanks to Kyle pouting and once again locking himself in his room. Taylor was taking a stroll through the retail heart of downtown when she came across a skirmish in the alley between the old-fashioned ice cream parlor and Yancy's by the Yard, a fabric emporium that specialized in locally made textiles, specialty yarns and hand-worked leathers.

Taylor eased between the onlookers, most of them tour-ists who'd been enjoying ice cream and cool drinks as they sat at the umbrella-adorned sidewalk café. Even before she was midway through the four-deep swarm of people, she recognized a familiar voice.

"You empty those pockets, boy," the owner of Ice 'n' Delights said sternly. Guy Graham had an opera tenor's rich voice, and beneath his immaculate white apron a body that could pass for one, too. "If Mrs. Yancy says you're the one who defaced her wall and trashed her place, you aren't going anywhere."

"Take a hike!" Kyle yelled back.

Although he had his back to her, Taylor could tell by the higher pitch in her son's voice that he wasn't as confident as he sounded. His hands were stuffed into his baggy jeans, and he kept glancing left and right as if expecting to be grabbed from behind.

"He's not big. I say you'n me grab a leg and turn him on his head, Mr. Graham." Another teen—obviously Guy's helper by the looks of the matching apron—looked eager for action standing at his boss's elbow. "We should be able to shake the truth out of him."

"Try it and you'll have to wear shades for a month," Kyle snarled, turning his baseball cap backward.

Seeing the stubborn gesture of attitude, Taylor decided not to wait for the scene to deteriorate any more. One person banged up in the family was enough. Wishing she could snatch her boy and vanish somewhere where no one had ever heard of the Bennings or even Redoubt, she approached the small standoff.

"That's enough threats. From everyone," she added as she stopped beside her son. She slid him a brief thanks-so-much glance.

Some paper refuse apparently from the ice cream parlor littered Madeline Yancy's whiskey barrel planters attractively adorned with red geraniums and assorted greenery. But what had Taylor wincing was the chalk cartoon on Madeline's red brick wall. It captured the petite entrepreneur perfectly, from her punkish short hairdo to her oversize eyeglasses and artist's smock…also her affection for very short leather skirts, the knobby knees that made them a questionable fashion choice and her rather voluptuous derriere.

Taylor recognized the impressive but misdirected talent immediately.

"Madeline." She focused on the offended woman who fancied herself the Edith Head of New Mexico. "Would you like to take a deep breath and tell me what happened?"

"You can see what happened," she cried shrilly. Maybe you'd better ask your son why it did."

She made a good point. The problem was that Taylor didn't trust herself to speak to her son just yet. It was clear now that he hadn't heard anything she'd told him when she'd announced they were moving back here, or during the drive across the country, or since their arrival. Not the crucial things.

"I'll tell you," Guy said, thrusting his chest out. "Your boy came in asking for a job. I told him that I didn't have anything behind the counter, being as young as he is, but if he wanted to be a busboy, he could start by cleaning up the alley. As you can see, the holiday crowd got a bit messy. Butch here was keeping an eye on him for me, showing him the routine, and I thought everything was going fine. Then all hell broke loose. I've never heard such yelling—and cussing!"

Nodding, Taylor eyed the older teen. She didn't recognize him, except that she had a feeling he was the son of one of the newer business people in town. A few years older than Kyle, she sensed a smugness that warned her to be especially careful in dealing with him.

"What's your full name, Butch?" she asked.

"My father's the new president of the bank."

He might as well have said, "...of the United States," and she couldn't have found a bigger ally of Murdock Marsden if she'd put an ad in the paper.

Taylor held the round-faced youth's gaze for several seconds before replying, "We didn't get to that question yet. What's your full name?"

The smugness vanished, replaced with resentment. "Cory Eugene Presser."

Kyle snorted.

Taylor lifted a finger. Her son bowed his head and shuffled an inch or two back.

"Just tell me what happened," she said to Butch.

"I came out here to do what Mr. Graham told me—to check on the kid. All I saw was trash everywhere."

"He's lying!" Kyle cried, lurching forward. "I had everything stacked and ready to be sacked when he came and threw it everywhere. Lardass is afraid he'll have to move his butt if there's someone around who actually earns their pay, yo."

Taylor didn't miss the "yo" that had been added on for Butch's benefit. It was the teenager-to-teenager shorthand to make a point that Kyle wasn't about to be intimidated by the bigger boy. As Butch fisted his hands and stepped toward him, Taylor shook her head, then redirected to Madeline.

"When you came out, all this was as you see it?"

"In the end. I mean, the first time the drawing wasn't there. He did it after I told him that I did not appreciate delinquents like him hanging around here where he had no business being. Kids come back here all the time to steal a quick smoke or heaven knows what else." Madeline lifted her chin. "To find out that one of the little monsters is yours makes me wonder what kind of justice we can expect around here, Taylor."

That's the lesson Kyle had refused to hear—that whatever he did, she would somehow pay for.

He shuffled, and fidgeted, and his breathing grew loud.

"She asked for it!" he shouted. "She never let me explain and made fun of my clothes. Who's she to talk? I wanted her to know what it's like."

"What were you thinking? You're too young to be holding down a steady job."

"I'm bored. You're too busy to get me the computer.

Gramps sleeps all the time, and there's no cable TV. I started to head for the feed store, but figured why bother? Mr. Dad-for-a-Day doesn't really want me. So I— What's the matter?''

Taylor couldn't believe it. Bad enough to show such poor judgment, not to mention poor behavior, but to choose now of all times to decide to call Hugh "Dad"...? She heard Madeline's gasp of surprise, and out of the corner of her eye saw Butch's curious glance slide from the woman to his boss. His puckish face took on a decided gleam of pleasure as he realized he'd fallen into important information. Taylor concluded the president of Redoubt First National would hear the news within minutes, and immediately afterward a call would be made to Murdock Marsden.

She had to warn Hugh. The air quality level around here was about to deteriorate in record time.

"We will talk. Later. In the meantime, you know what you have to do." She looked at Madeline Yancy again, whom she'd known since they were in home ec together and had both flunked cooking. It looked as though Madeline preferred to forget the connection. "May Kyle borrow a bucket of soaped water and a brush?"

"With pleasure."

There was no time to let her ex-schoolmate's haughtiness upset her. She crooked a finger to Butch, who saw the change in the adults around him and approached with more curiosity than fear.

"Let's understand each other," she told him, her smile crisp. "You have gotten away with nothing. Your father will hear about the trouble you helped cause here, regardless of what tales you spin to the contrary. In the meantime, if I hear you've tried to pull another stunt, we will meet again. Understood?"

"Whatever. If you're still around by then."

That was what she had to look forward to from here on out. Days ago when she had learned Hugh was home, she understood that the news would get out. She supposed she should be grateful that things had stayed quiet as long as they had.

"Little boy," she said so softly only he could hear. "Count on it."

By the time she got to the feed store, the news had already reached Hugh.

"Mel phoned. He thought I should know." He led her into the office in case someone came by or was watching them from across the street. "I'm just relieved my mother's still in Arizona."

Poor Noel was having troubles of her own. It had turned out that after all these years, she'd fallen in love with none other than the mysterious but charismatic benefactor of the women's refuge center where she worked, of all places, a man she had known for years, had learned to trust, only to find out he'd once hurt a woman himself.

Hugh had made it clear to his mother that she should stay as long as Noel needed her.

"I'm glad, too. And I'm sorry about this, Hugh. The timing…"

"Shh." He drew her into his arms and kissed her near the smaller bandage she now wore over her cut. "We knew it would happen. How are you holding up? I hear Kyle pulled a good one."

"He's managed to establish himself as Redoubt's first gang member. How do you think I'm holding up?"

"I didn't know he drew."

"It's an on-again, off-again passion, if that makes any sense. I've tried to encourage him ever since a teacher told me that he has tremendous potential. Unfortunately, most of the examples I've gotten to see of it are on the sides of buildings like today. And the sad thing is that anytime something goes wrong for him, the first thing he does is deny himself his art. It kills me to have to punish him on top of that—and I should have found that half day to get him that computer I've promised him. He might be a cyber junkie by now, but at least he wouldn't be in the middle of this mess."

"Stop beating yourself up." Hugh tucked her head under his chin and stroked her back. "You've been both mother and father to him, and from what I can see, you've done a terrific job. He's bright, damn fine looking—" his chest shook as she punched him lightly in the ribs "—and beneath the attitude is a boy searching for direction on how to be a man. It was my job to be that rudder. I failed both of you."

"Now who's beating themselves up? But you know what he did say? He'd almost come here. He just lost his nerve."

"I scared him off by being a disciplinarian too quickly. My people skills are rough, Blue."

"No one gets it right all the time. You've always had great instincts. Keep trusting them."

Her own instincts weren't off much about how long it would take for Murdock Marsden to contact her. She got a call from her father that the scion had phoned in a fury amid a number of other calls demanding for her immediate discharge.

"On what grounds?" she demanded. She already knew what he would say, but she needed the adrenaline charge.

"The war drums'll be going tonight, daughter. Can you hold it together?"

Taylor knew of only one answer to give him. "I have to, don't I?"

Hugh was relieved to be able to shut the warehouse doors that night. The store had experienced more traffic in the hours after Taylor left than in the week thus far. Unfortunately, few had been customers.

It wasn't all bad, though. A few old-timers and former classmates wandered in with sheepish smiles and strong handshakes.

"I'd wondered," was the typical comment. "I'd been hoping. There is justice, after all."

Besides Mel, there was Steve Canton and Chris Hutton. Those were the guys who made the critics and bigots ignorable. Schoolmates who'd stood by him during his trial, they were glad to hear he and Taylor hadn't missed out completely. At the same time, no one was about to step out on Main Street and publicly announce again that they thought he'd been framed fourteen years ago—they all had businesses in the community now that relied on local support, and few had Taylor's depth of character. But to have them no longer avoiding him helped.

Naturally, the others did not need to look him in the eye to deliver their messages, and those were succinct. He received a few calls where someone whispered, "Murderer," and hung up, or "Your bastard's no more welcome here than you are!" Nevertheless, there weren't as many as he felt there might have been, and he hoped that Taylor was finding that to be the case, too.

It stayed incredibly hot after the sun went down, and more humid than usual. The southwest's monsoon season was about to start, and none too soon. The humid heat compelled Hugh to pull a chair out onto the dock and watch the stars. It was a particularly pleasurable fantasy that Taylor might be able to stop by. Since he hadn't heard from her after this morning's visit, he figured she had her hands full, but a guy could hope. It had been almost a week since they'd made love. That too-brief taste of what life could be was like being teased with a teaspoon of water in a desert. Yes, Taylor made him dream...and worry.

Debating on whether or not to venture out to the Benning residence, he was slow to pick up on the smell of smoke until he actually saw the trail coming over the roof of the warehouse. Leaping off the dock, he ran out into the middle of the parking lot and saw the denser cloud of smoke immediately on the back side of his own building!

Swearing, Hugh ran.

Eight

"So I yelled to my girlfriend to phone the fire department and then I followed Hugh back here."

Taylor listened calmly, but she couldn't believe the scene that lay before her. Illuminated by the security lights on utility poles in the area, smoke continued to rise from the ground around Jane Blackstone's trailer as well as the rear of the feed store, but at least the flames were out. What a blessing that both structures were constructed of metal and not wood, otherwise the damage would have been far more severe. Shaking her head, she focused at the back of the office area of the store that Tito Hernandez was pointing to.

"That's where most of the papers were thrown. They smelled soaked with kerosene to me."

"You're sure?"

"We were poor when I was a kid back in Mexico. We were lucky to have any kind of fuel and if we got some that was it. You don't forget."

"And you didn't see anyone around?"

"Well, there were a few people coming down the back alley because they saw the smoke and fire, too. One came with a fire extinguisher, another with a shovel. Mr. Montez, Sr., drove the tractor down with the front bucket full of sand and put out that section."

He pointed to where a grass fire had been stopped. Had it continued, the small hardware and lumber business next door could have been next to be ignited. All the names Tito had mentioned were people with more commercial types of businesses, the less photogenic businesses that the retailers depended on to keep their stores operational, and area residents depended on for their utilitarian needs. Most still stood around because what they were looking at painted the disturbing picture of arson.

She hadn't been inside either the trailer or store yet to see how bad the damage was—if any. From the looks of things, except for some wiring and cosmetic damage, the Blackstones were still in business. If she hadn't been inspecting Kyle's cleaning job to reassure Madeline Yancy that she had no intention of showing special considerations to her son, she would have been here sooner. Gus had been playing his outside stereo quite loud, and as a result, she hadn't heard the fire engine sirens on the other end of town.

"But no one...stood out? No one who didn't belong around here?"

"Before long there were lots of people from all over town who never come down here." The trim Hispanic wiped at his thick mustache that had to be as caked with soot and dust as the rest of him. "I tell you, Officer Benning, I don't mess with nobody's business, but we all watch for one another on this end of town and we'll keep an eye on the place until he comes back, but—" he pointed to the unstructured group of eight or ten standing on the far side of the alley "—I got no use for that kind. Some of 'em came in time, they could have helped. Look at 'em.

They weren't about to dirty their hands, and most of 'em never met Hugh before. How can they judge him?''

"I don't know, Tito, but I'm grateful you think the way you do, and I'd like you to call me Taylor." She put out her hand, which, after a startled glance, he enthusiastically accepted. "You're sure Hugh didn't say where he was heading?"

"Not to me. He was shook up, though, I can tell you that.''

Thanking him again, Taylor headed back to her father's Blazer. She was about to telephone the house to see if perhaps Hugh had gone there to look for her when Mel rounded the front of the truck.

"I've been looking for you!" Gasping he pointed west. "Hugh's going after Lew Sandoval. Somebody mentioned seeing Sandoval at the gas station and laughing over the fire, and Hugh just took off.''

"Thanks.''

Taylor scrambled into the truck, ignoring the cry from the reporter representing the county paper whom she'd promised an interview to. She would have to apologize later and see what she could do to make up for breaking her word, but this was more important.

She had no idea where she was going, except to start at the convenience store/gas station at the west end of town. But she prayed that Hugh didn't do anything foolish. Just because Lew was enjoying the Blackstone's streak of bad luck didn't mean the guy had set the fires. Did she think so? It was probable, but she couldn't arrest him on a hunch. On the other hand, Hugh could go back to jail if Lew filed charges of assault against him.

Neither man was at the station, but the two young men attending it knew of Lew and told her that he had indeed been there, and that barely a minute or so after he left, heading back toward the MP, a man matching Hugh's description arrived asking about him.

Back on the road again, Taylor was aware that at this

point she should be advising her father that she was about to be out of the city limits. But he would urge her to call the sheriff's office. She wasn't about to do that when she didn't know what Hugh had gotten himself into.

About five miles down the road, she saw two trucks stopped half on and half off the road. Because their engines were still running and their lights were on, she could see them in the throes of one serious fight. She decided against kicking on her overhead lights, but as soon as she climbed out of the truck, she pulled her gun and shot a round into the air.

"That's it! Knock it off!"

Hugh took advantage as Lew hesitated and with a right cross knocked him to the asphalt.

"Hugh! Damn it, Blackstone...have you lost all of your senses? Don't even think it, Lew," she added as the older man began reaching into his boot. She kept them both in her sights. "You two stay where you are. Lew, very slowly, take out the knife and slide it this way."

At first it looked as though he might defy her, but with a sneering smile, he tugged at his jeans and reached into his left boot, tossing an expensive-looking lock-back knife toward her. Slowly pocketing it, Taylor gestured to his truck where a hunting rifle hung in the window rack.

"Is that all you're carrying?"

"Yeah."

"And since I believe you, lift your other pant leg."

Muttering an obscenity, he jerked at it. "Want me to unzip my pants next?"

"That's all right." She circled both men to Lew's truck. "I'm depressed enough as it is."

She found a handgun in the door compartment of the pickup. Tucking it into the waistband of her jeans, she lifted the rifle from the rack. "You'll get these back after you cool off and come into the station and tell me why you couldn't have had anything to do with the fire."

"You can't do that."

"Or I can arrest you now, and you can go through the trouble of phoning Murdock Marsden, asking him to send a lawyer for you. How do you think he's going to like being embarrassed that way?"

"Embarrassed over what? A false arrest?"

"No...I have witnesses who say you've been stealing gas and other things from the convenience store for a long time. Amazing. Too cheap to pay for a candy bar, Lew? Does that really make you feel like a big man?" She planned to have a chat with her father about all that later. "I don't know what it's like for ex-cops in prison down here, Lew, but up north it's said to be quite an experience."

He rose from the ground with impressive speed for someone who looked as though he'd taken the worst of the beating. "You—"

"Shut up, you pig!" Hugh lunged toward him.

"Hugh!" Taylor made the rifle a line between them. When she saw him clench his fists and knew he could be trusted to be still another moment or two, she said to Lew, "Get moving. While you still can."

He didn't need a second invitation, and did his best to kick up as much gravel and dust as he could as he sped down the road. Taylor watched until the lights of his truck disappeared over one hill and high on another. Finally, she let herself breathe, really breathe, and put Lew's weighty hardware in the Blazer.

Hugh had kept his eyes on the twin red lights until they were completely out of sight. When she stopped behind him, he turned. It was a moment too big for words.

She didn't know how he could have risked this after what they'd endured all these years. Shaking her head, she reached for him in the same instant he reached for her. They clung in the nimbus of white lights, and farther beyond the stars twinkled...a little less out of reach than usual.

Her emotions swinging like a pendulum from relief to

frustration, Taylor gripped two handfuls of his shirt and demanded, "What did you think you were going to prove going out after him alone like that?"

"I wasn't trying to prove anything."

She let herself finally focus on his face and, wincing, cupped the high cheekbone that was so swollen it looked ready to erupt. And his hands... When he closed his hands over her wrists, she saw the bloody knuckles; she moaned, her own hands throbbing in empathy.

"It's all right. I don't think I broke anything."

"You could have been killed!"

"Me? What about you? My God, you were feral. You were...you were wonderful," he said, murmuring the last as he ducked to close his mouth over hers.

She wasn't finished giving him a piece of her mind, but having him close, and safe, was more important. In case he was hurt elsewhere, she wanted to be gentle. He wanted roughness, and his kiss was wild and hungry. In the end it was all right with her, too, and she rose on tiptoe and tried to give him all he wanted. Maybe, she thought, maybe if she loved him well enough, she could keep him safe.

An owl screeched up in the trees to their north, reminding them where they were. It had Hugh throwing back his head and yelling back, "When!"

"Hugh, you're hurt, and exhausted. Come back to town with me."

He didn't budge. "When's it going to be our time, Blue? There's no end to it."

"You've only been home a short time. We'll find answers."

"Will there be anything left?"

As exhausted as she was, Taylor ignored her own fatigue to buffer him. "The fire didn't do serious damage, Hugh. Hold on to that. Either whoever did it wasn't very knowledgeable about fires or being in a hurry was the chief requisite."

"We know the 'whoever.'"

"We have no witness, and he didn't confess." She took his bruised, soot-and-dirt-stained hand and coaxed him to his truck. "*Please*. Come home with me. Dad would want you to."

"I can't do that."

"You can't go back to that...that cave! Even if it was safe, the lingering smell of smoke will make you sick to your stomach. Most important, I won't lose you again," she said fiercely. "And I know what kind of demons take hold when you're alone in the dark too much."

He seemed appreciative of that, and yet he remained hesitant. "I'm concerned that someone might try something or to play scavenger. Almost everyone knows my mother is out of town. If I'm not around to keep an eye on the place—"

"I'll go string yellow tape around the back. The insurance people will need to see that when they come out to inspect the place, anyway."

"I can't let you do all that by yourself. I'll go with you."

Taylor vetoed that outright. "I want you out of sight. Come on, Blackstone. I'm not going to make you do this yourself. I'll follow you to the house and explain things to Dad before I go take care of the rest."

"Under one condition. If Emmett prefers I disappear— either because he's concerned for you, or for his job—I'm out of there."

Taylor didn't bother replying. Why agree to something that wasn't going to happen?

Hugh remained dubious as he followed Taylor into her family home, but not only was Emmett relieved to see his daughter home safe, he gave Hugh what seemed a genuinely warm handshake.

"You look as though you settled at least one or two scores," he told him.

"Well, I got started, anyway."

"Dad, there's no way Hugh should go back to the store tonight. I said he could stay here, okay?"

"You have to ask? Hugh, go on, get yourself some ice and a beer from the kitchen." Emmett held up his empty can. "And bring me a refill, too."

Taylor leaned over the back of the couch and patted his belly, but when she spoke she asked, "How's Kyle?"

"He knows you're taking a lot of heat for him. The phone's been ringing off the wall. Never imagined one kid could turn so many folks into 'concerned citizens.' And when Lola called about the fire, which I'd like to point out neither I nor Orrin had been informed of—ahem—"

"Dad, I was racing to get there, and then when I went after Hugh, I didn't want you to worry."

"Your boy's the one who was worried."

Taylor frowned. "He knows what my work is like."

"He knows what a city cop's work is like, where you worked with a partner, backup. Here, you're on your own. He thought he was getting Snooze City, U.S.A., instead he's seen a demolished patrol car, you all beat up, after being shot at..."

"Chief, are you suggesting I can't handle the job?"

"...and now just when he's thinking about how cool it might be to have an old man," her father drawled, shifting wise and troubled eyes at Hugh, "someone tries to burn you out, and you come in looking as if you went through the same grinder she did." He pointed the remote control to turn down the TV so he could keep his voice low. "If you think he's just worried about losing both of his parents, now that he's finally got a set like other kids he used to make fun of, try this one on for size. He asked me if I thought you might crack this time if you had to shoot to kill again."

Taylor pressed a hand to her eyes, a movement that would have had Hugh across the room in a second if Emmett hadn't signaled for him to stay put. It turned out that he knew his daughter best. She did blink hard as she glanced upstairs, but it was the front door she aimed for.

"I'll be back as soon as I take care of things at the store," she said quietly.

Wanting badly to go after her, Hugh waited only long enough for the door to shut behind her before demanding of Emmett, "Tell me."

"She should do that herself."

"Well, that's not likely to happen, is it?" He dropped down on the chair beside the suddenly drained cop. "Hell, Emmett, I know there's no reason for you to like me, let alone want me around Taylor..."

"She loves you, has all her life. The dumbest thing you ever did was punish her, and punish yourself by not fighting for that."

"You know Murdock was going to see that someone paid, and if it wasn't going to be the real murderer, then it was going to be the guy who left him dazed on the ground."

"Yeah. Yeah, I guess you're right." Sighing, Emmett gestured toward the kitchen again. "Go get that ice and those beers and I'll tell you what you want to know. Then you go upstairs and see your boy. Marsden's stolen enough from my grandson."

Almost a half hour later Hugh knocked at his son's door. He was thinking about an opening line when he heard the boy.

"Mom! Listen, Mom, I didn't mean to—" the door swung open "—jeez."

"Hi. Want some company?"

The teen's soft features grew wary. "Is this round two even before Mom strikes with round one?"

"No, this is your lucky day. Your critical mass has been replaced with mine." As expected, the boy's face screwed up like an infant tasting anything sour for the first time.

"I guess I don't have your mother's ability to tell a joke. What I meant was—"

Kyle almost succeeded in getting one side of his mouth to curl. "No, I, uh, get it. I heard about the fire. Is that why you're here? Are you moving in?"

Hugh wished he could tell whether the boy was projecting desire or despair? It amazed him that he'd known Taylor, known her feelings almost as well as his own, and yet here stood the results of those feelings, and his perceptions were muddled in static.

"Don't panic, the damage is contained to the outside, but the smoke's left the place uninhabitable for a while." Hugh nodded down the hall. "Your grandfather's allowing me to use his room. Is that going to be okay with you?"

It didn't take ESP to see that the boy didn't expect anyone to ask for his approval.

"Yeah." His nod grew increasingly stronger. "It's a stoopid idea."

"Wh— Come again?"

"Two O's...like in good."

"Interesting."

"Guess you didn't hear much teen slang where you were." As soon as the words were out, Kyle grimaced. "Mom would be gagging if she heard me say that. Sorry."

"No, need. That's where I was. As for the language in prison...well, let's just say she'd be ten times more upset to hear you speaking it."

Hugh allowed himself a peek into the room. He expected seeing a mess that would make a parent shudder and refuse to enter. Except for wall-to-wall posters, though, and the mass of papers on the bed, the room looked relatively neat.

"Can I ask you something?"

He focused on his son. "Sure."

"How'd you get that?" Kyle pointed to his own right cheekbone.

"Left hook. I chased down the guy I think started the fire."

"Butters, man."

"Is that something like a thumbs-up?"

Kyle grinned. "Two of them." Then he grew sober. "Is Mom okay? Where is she? Booking him?"

"Ah, no. We had to let him go. Lack of evidence."

"Lawyers. Mom says they're about as useful as nuclear waste."

Kyle had said the word in the same way Hugh's mother said "taxes." Hugh coughed lightly. "Your mother's doing some last minute things. She'll be in any minute."

"You think she's still mad about what I did today? Did Gramps tell her about all the calls he's been getting?"

"He mentioned them."

The boy grew troubled. "I don't know why I let my temper get the best of me."

"Believe me, it happens." Hugh thought of something and decided to go with it. "I hope you inherited your mother's disposition instead of mine. But it's important to understand that everyone gets upset occasionally. The trick is to process it into something constructive, not destructive. From what I hear, though, you were on the right track. If you'd have been a decade or so older and had drawn your caricature on paper and signed it, I'll bet Madeline Yancy would have been highly flattered."

"Yeah?"

"Absolutely." He decided to take another chance. "Is that some of your work?" he asked, nodding to the papers on the bed. "May I look?"

His son stepped aside to let him enter, but as he followed he said, "I'm not trained or anything. I just mess around sometimes."

Hugh wandered around the full-sized bed, careful how he drew out one sheet from another. That's when the boy saw his knuckles.

"Damn. Your hands! I mean—"

"No, I've been thinking a few colorful things myself as the throbbing has set in. And I'm not picking anything up because I don't want to make a mess on any of this. But you're... I don't know what to say. You seem so young to be so creative. I'm impressed, Kyle."

It wasn't going to be that easy. While Kyle didn't look unpleased at being praised, it seemed as though he was also intent on downplaying its value to him. It hurt, but Hugh didn't allow himself to shut down his emotions as he did while incarcerated. If he wanted a chance at playing at least a minimal role in this boy's life, he didn't dare be stingy with what was going on inside himself.

He took a deep breath. "It's all right, you know."

"What is?"

"Wanting to reject me. You've had it rough enough without finding out that of all the guys who could be your father, it's a convicted murderer."

Kyle couldn't bring himself to meet his gaze, but the boy shrugged, shifted, fought. "Mom doesn't think you are."

Hugh could see he wanted to believe, but feared trusting yet again. How many times, how many people, had let this child down? How could a world build healthy, productive inhabitants if the primary lesson every child learned was never trust?

"I'm not," he said quietly but clearly. "You were not sired by a murderer. I'm not saying I didn't have the rage or hate to want to kill Piers Marsden that day, but I swear to you...on the most precious thing I can, which is the love I held for your mother, I did not do it."

The boy's chin trembled. Hugh couldn't see his eyes because his lashes, as long and thick as his mother's, hid them. But when he extended his arms, he knew he was doing the right thing.

Kyle launched himself across the room.

Filthy from fighting the fire and sore from taking on that pit bull Sandoval, Hugh had many reasons to wince at how hard the boy held him. But the burning in his eyes had nothing to do with any of that. As he hugged Kyle in return, he could barely contain the joy at being able to experience such a connection even for a moment.

"It's not fair," Kyle mumbled.

"No. But it's getting better."

"Everybody hates us here. And I hate them!"

"Not everybody. And you don't, either." Hugh stroked the boy's mussed hair, so black and shiny, and he had a sudden flashback of his father doing the same thing to him the day he'd been given an adult's wallet with a ten-dollar bill inside. It had been his birthday—exactly a week before his father was killed. What a symbol that gift had proven to be, and how he hoped his father had felt half this good that day.

"I'm scared."

Ah. He knew about fear. "It's okay to admit that. But we can't run from it."

"I don't want to stay here. Not if Mom and you aren't safe."

This was what Emmett had explained, and Hugh could offer no empty guarantees. It made thinking of a reply difficult. "Your mother gave her word, though, didn't she? You know how she is about that?" Feeling the boy nod, he continued, "And I can't run, Kyle. Someone here stole important things from me—my freedom, my good name, my *family*. I have to try to get them back."

When he left Kyle's room and continued down the hall, Hugh was feeling more than a little light-headed. His expectations about coming here had been nominal and modest at that. Right now, the only thing more he could ask for was to know that Taylor was back in the house for the night, and he could lay his head on a pillow and sleep for a week.

Emmett's room was large, which was necessary for the huge furnishings, but those were few and the effect was uncluttered, except for the photos on the bureau. As he unbuttoned his soot-and-bloodstained shirt, he studied each—pictures of Taylor at various stages of her life, some with her father, most alone. Hugh picked up the one from her senior prom. He'd taken her, and the photo was of them together. They'd been so young, so full of confidence and love. What he felt for her now was no less exciting— and it wasn't just sex, although he accepted that Taylor was always going to be it for him—but there was a deeper appreciation of who she'd been, who she'd had to be in order to survive and accomplish all that she had. Damn, but she was something else.

Moving the silver-framed photo to the nighttable, he went into the bathroom and, turning on the light, considered himself in the harsh light. He no longer bore any resemblance to that naive kid in the photo. Anger, hate...life itself had broken off his softer edges not rubbed, chiseled or hammered them off. He lived with the tension of a predator thrumming inside him and looked older, harder, than his father had the last time he'd seen him. What on earth did Taylor see that she should still want him?

Hurry home, Blue. I need to see your eyes.

He was letting the hot shower spray soothe his overtight muscles when her slender arms came gliding around him, her sleek body pressed against his back. Certain he was imagining her, even though he heard her murmur, "Feel better?", he had to turn around to make sure.

"Now that you're here." He brought her fully against him again, his body growing instantly alert as to what preciousness it held. Aching for more of her softness, he rubbed his cheek against hers, adding, "Everything all right?"

"Seems to be. The town's quiet."

She, too, seemed restless and nuzzled his ear with her nose, kissed a spot on the side of his neck where he felt his pulse beating hard and fast.

"Kyle tells me you two had a talk."

"He let me hold him."

"He said he called you 'Dad' when you said good-night."

Emotion clamped a vise around his throat as it had then, and he held her all the tighter against his heart. "He's wonderful. And you're wonderful," he said, seeking her mouth with his.

He found it and brushed his lips against hers, nudged them open and nibbled. Even when he needed more, needed the sexy glide of their tongues taking turns sheathing each other, he was careful to be tender. He wanted to thank her for having done such a great job raising their son, for being more than anything he deserved, for giving him back his will to live. He tried to pour it all into his kiss, and she did respond, her body arching to get closer to his, her hands eloquently transmitting appreciation and encouragement as they moved from his shoulders to his hips. But it wasn't enough. Yet when in her generosity she moved to caress his turgid length, he shifted out of her reach because he had more to say.

He moved on to the apple breasts he adored, the rosy nipples from which her child had nursed. The steamy water had already wet and warmed her, but it was his mouth that won soft purring sounds from deep in her throat.

Sinking to his knees, he rubbed his cheek against where his seed had grown into embryo and fetus. He'd missed it all—those first miraculous flutters of life, the mysterious alluring changes of her body, the baby's feisty arrival.... He'd offered no back rubs to ease her, no strength to sustain her through labor, no night watch so she could sleep and regain her energy. He owed her everything, and all he had to offer her was his love.

In homage he ventured lower. Already sensing her tense and tighten the fingers gripping his shoulders, he hoped what he had to give was enough.

"Let me, sweetheart," he said, planting coaxing kisses on one silky thigh, then the other. He was asking for her trust now. She'd forgotten how to give herself completely, to yield control, and he wanted her to rediscover there was a gift in it, just as he wanted the someone she trusted to be him.

"Let me, love," he murmured, opening his mouth over her. And then he did what time had only allowed them once, before they'd been torn from each other's life; he gave her what he knew he would never be tempted to give anyone else, and sought what he'd been fantasizing for countless days and nights.

Understandably, she resisted more, her hands shifting into his hair. But he did know her after all, understood the deepest parts of her that responded to his gentling touch, his slower caresses. His heart swelled as she grew pliant and when she stroked the water-slick sweep of his hair, urged him closer, he knew the last of the walls that were separating them had crumbled at last.

"Please…" she gasped.

"As much as you want," he murmured against her. "For as long as you'll have me."

Nine

Taylor couldn't stop trembling even after Hugh carried her from the bathroom and lowered her onto the bed. It was as if she was part of some tremendous electrical circuit that she couldn't break free of. But then she didn't want to be free.

Hugh stretched out beside her, his powerful body no dryer than hers and radiating a heat that made her feel as though they were still standing under the hot spray of the shower.

"All right?"

His voice was as gentle as the thumb stroking moisture off her cheek. He wasn't missing any opportunity to touch her, but he didn't seem in a hurry to complete their intimate connection, either.

A quick turn of her head allowed her to press a kiss into his cupped palm. "I will be when you're inside me again."

Fire burned in his eyes, and his body's reaction spoke

of a not-so-controlled restraint. "Soon. Let me look at you first. Do you know what a luxury that is?"

"You're doing a lovely job convincing me."

"And you're simply lovely. It breaks my heart to know you've let yourself forget that."

Not wanting him to be upset with her, she stretched to kiss the bruise on his cheek. "Right now I don't know which of us would make the better cover model for a hockey magazine."

"I know who'd I'd vote for," he replied, his gaze sweeping down her naked length. "Provided I got the only copy."

This was the Hugh Thomas Blackstone who'd taught her about love and being a woman, the big, hawk-eyed cowboy who'd made her feel like Miss America, a centerfold playmate and an angel all at once. How did she tell him that although there were moments over the years that she wouldn't have missed for the world—almost all of them having to do with Kyle—her world had been so lonely without him.

He must have seen it in her eyes. His narrowed. "What's wrong?"

"Nothing." She smiled, pushed him flat on his back and rose above him. "I'll show you."

She wanted to give him himself back, too. There was no way she could make up for every day of isolation he'd suffered, the lost days in the sun and all the laughter, his share of hugs denied...missed sacred moments. She was too late to soothe the scars she could see on his warrior's body or those that were hidden from human eyes. But she could show him that all of that had changed nothing—just as he'd shown her.

He'd always loved her hands on him. She splayed her fingers wide and refamiliarized herself with the body she'd once known as well as her own. Maturity and strength had made him more beautiful, but then he had always brought out the sensualist in her. Even the scars—although thoughts of how he'd gotten them tormented her—were part of the sum total of who he'd become. From shoulder to breast, from ribs to the hard cords of his flat belly, she caressed him.

But hands weren't enough. She began all over again with her mouth.

"Blue..."

She lingered on his nipples, enjoying the change in his breathing, the way he stroked her hair when she felt a need burning inside him to do something far more fierce. It was what drove his fever and had him straining as she nuzzled the arrow of hair that led to his painfully erect flesh.

Just the shift of air as her breath touched him won a soft moan. When she kissed him, he barely bit back a tortured cry.

"No, sweetheart. Blue, no. I can't."

"But I want this."

His grip was merciless as he stopped her again. "Damn it—I'll lose it!"

What she heard was, "I'll disappoint you."

The tender smile in her eyes and a kiss for each forearm was all it took for him to release her. "What is it you say to me? 'As much as you want. For as long as you'll have me,'" she murmured. "How can you think it's any different for me?"

His hand trembled as his thumb stroked across her lower lip. His searing gaze said, "Then take me. Love me. And don't ever stop."

Her name was a ragged sigh as she encircled him with her mouth. Not an inch of him remained uninvolved; his hands, his entire body, trembled with repressed longing, and soon his breathing grew into a harsh soliloquy of bittersweet torment.

Taylor had never felt so strong and yet so protective in her life. What she lacked in experience, she made up for by simply cherishing him, until he came apart under her loving ministrations. Then, when he finally calmed to where his breathing had at least slowed to a soft pant, she rose over him and began to arouse him again with caresses from her entire body.

His gaze, overbright and intense, held hers as she slowly sank onto him, held it still as they absorbed the sensations of sheathing and being sheathed by her moist heat. And just as she saw his Adam's apple move against a dry swallow, she slowly, slowly, began an age-old dance that took him deeper and deeper.

He encouraged her in so many ways—with his adoring eyes, his hands stroking her thighs, his thumbs stroking the V bisecting leg from hip, his callused palms sensitizing her already taut breasts, until her nipples throbbed with hunger.

Leaning closer she whispered, "Kiss me...wet me."

With a groan he took her into his mouth, his tongue and lips both gentling and instigating, and all the while the rocking went on like the relentless tide.

By the time her own body was screaming for release, his was, too. Almost simultaneously, as her movements and his answering thrusts became more forceful, he drew her down for a kiss equally fierce.

The urgency mounted, becoming a fist in her abdomen, a pounding in her ears. Unable to get enough air into her lungs, she reared back and, gasping, rode him hard. As his fingers bit almost painfully into her hips, she felt the eruption. The subtle shock of him pouring into her sensitive flesh triggered her own spasms, and, shuddering, she let Hugh tug her into his viselike embrace.

He stared up at the ceiling. He and Taylor hadn't said a word for several minutes, partly because this last climax on top of everything else they'd shared tonight had left them temporarily drained. But he also knew she was waiting for what he'd already shown her, had intimated through endearments, but hadn't completely let her own again.

As if you don't already know she's always owned the words.

"I love you," he said, his voice sounding rusty even to him.

She shifted to her side and rose on her left elbow. Her gaze was tender, but she didn't smile. "I love you back. But I think saying it and...yes, hearing it is still a problem for you. Can you tell me why?"

"You have to ask? There's too much unfinished business lying ahead of us."

"We'll deal with it."

"Will we?" Hugh wished he could match her conviction. But even if they did make it, that just brought them to the point where most couples start.

As if reading his mind, Taylor stroked his chest hairs, a tiny smile playing around her mouth. "You mean, I give you a son, I may even be carrying your second—or a daughter—and you still don't want to make an honest woman out of me?"

He swore viciously, pressing his palms into his eye sockets. "You see what I mean? I should be shot for not taking care of you. Years ago was bad enough, but at least I could use youth and raging hormones as a half-baked excuse."

"Your hormones weren't raging the last two times we've made love?"

This was why he'd never stood a chance. She could go from dead serious to sexy seductress to sweet dream in a heartbeat, and while he would be trying to catch up, she'd been wrapping his heartstrings in knots. It shook him to realize that all those years of incarceration hadn't disciplined him one bit, at least not where she was concerned.

With a feral growl, he rolled her onto her back and kept her there with his much more substantial weight. "My hormones were a mess all five times, Blue. That's the problem."

"Yes, but two were no-risk bonuses," she murmured, her eyes sparkling.

Heaven help him. "No risk to you, maybe, but I can't say the same for my sanity. Wanting you is a disease in my blood." Even now he wanted to kiss her breathless, slide into her again and watch her burn for him. "But what if the world turns inside out again? Do you think I'm going to let them lock me away from you and Kyle? The mere thought that you could go through a whole other pregnancy alone— I'd go out of my mind, Blue."

Taylor stroked his face and chest. "Shh...it's not going to happen."

"What? Do you have a crystal ball that I don't know about? It didn't do so well warning you about someone trying to kill you!"

"I'm beginning to believe that we were allowed to be together again for a reason, Hugh, and not to lose everything in one tragic moment."

She couldn't know how badly he wanted to believe that, but his mind was on a perverse bent. "Right. The fates probably prefer I watch your love for me die slowly as you deal with the fact that you've tied yourself to a man with nothing to show for his life but a black mark on his reputation."

"Hugh."

"I don't even have a job."

"Of course you do!"

"Hauling sacks of feed at a farm supply store that you could inventory in an hour is not my idea of a career."

"Then go to school as we always planned."

"Taylor, damn it, do you think I could have stayed sane sitting in a cell all those years doing nothing but pumping iron? I did go to school, and I have a degree in law! But do you think they're going to let a convicted murderer take the state bar exam?"

"So we'll appeal your conviction." Taylor's smile was radiant. "Hugh, that's wonderful! I'm beyond words proud of you! In the meantime I can support us," she continued excitedly. "We don't need much, and I have some savings outside of Kyle's school fund. I know Dad will welcome us here. He'll probably insist we take this room."

Yes, she loved him. The knowledge left him as humbled as it did euphoric. But she was nowhere near the realist that he was. "Blue...and what if you have to pull your gun to really use it again?" Seeing her eyes darken with pain, he wanted to crush her against him and beg her to forgive him for bringing up the memory; nevertheless, he had to say what she refused to face. "I made your father tell me."

"He had no right to."

"You intended to keep it a secret?"

"It's not a secret, it's..." With a sigh, she draped her arm over her eyes. "It's history, Hugh."

"You almost took a bullet to save someone who was more than willing to kill you!"

"He was twelve years old!"

"He was a heroin addict aiming a loaded gun at you!" Instead of following her training and instincts, Emmett had told him, she'd tried to reason with the boy. Her hesitation almost cost her her life, because when she realized he was beyond hearing her, she'd barely beat him on the trigger, sending his bullet into the wall next to her neck.

"I kept seeing Kyle," she said, her voice emotionless. "I saw myself answering the door and seeing two police officers there to tell me that my child was dead."

"Kyle told his grandfather that you cried for days."

"I got help."

"You still get nightmares."

"You don't?"

"But I'm not the one wearing the badge in this town, Taylor."

Taylor muttered an unladylike expletive and rolled off the bed. "Damn it, Hugh, get off my case! Why are you doing this to us?"

"Because history does sometimes repeat itself. Because I'm terrified at how you may react if we do find out who killed Piers and who's behind all of this mess. What if it's someone you know?"

"It won't matter."

Hugh sprang off the bed and snatched the shirt she'd reached for. "How do you know that?" he demanded, his voice shaking with the same quiet fury hers did.

"Because I love you and nothing, *nothing*, is going to get between us again, you—"

He didn't let her finish. His emotions as explosive as hers, he snaked an arm around her waist and clamped his other hand to the back of her head, then crushed his mouth to hers.

She was magnificent. With the same strength she'd fought for her sanity, she fought for their love. He couldn't hold her close enough or get enough of the passion that radiated from her kisses like a fever.

"Forgive me," he whispered, pressing his mouth to her throat. "But I had to know you can handle it. Taylor...love...don't you know it would kill me to know I caused you pain like that again?"

She let her body relax against his. She was less quick to answer, but when she did, she began by pressing a kiss to where his heart beat hardest. "Few police officers get through their careers without a few stressful incidents. What offsets that is the satisfaction of knowing you help. You help in a huge way. I love what I do, Hugh...and I love you and Kyle. Why can't you try to accept that?"

He had to learn to try. "Bear with me?" he asked with a sheepish smile.

Not surprisingly, a wicked light lit her eyes. She shifted again to take his stubborn arousal into the protective juncture of her silky-smooth thighs. "Make it worth my while."

"Sweet heaven..." Hugh whispered, backing her toward the bed again.

* * *

As far as Taylor was concerned, their lives began that night, and despite getting very little sleep, she bounced out of bed early the next morning and nearly flew out of the house. Even the irate calls from the mayor and others that were either waiting for her as she arrived at the station or kept the phone lines busy all morning as word spread about Kyle's paternity and the Blackstones' latest trouble didn't begin to dampen her happiness. That wasn't to say it wasn't demanding work to stay reasonable and cheerful. As a result, when Mel phoned in the late morning and told her that he'd come upon a litter of pups needing a home, she thought it as good a time as any to take a break.

After phoning Kyle to let him know she would be picking him up in a minute, she went out to Orrin. "Orrin, have you seen the Blackstone file I had on the office desk? I thought I'd take it home to the chief."

Ducking his head into his shoulders as he always did when embarrassed, Orrin rose and picked it up from his desk. "Here it is."

Taylor's smile faltered. "Why do you have it?"

"I thought I would read it when you weren't. Thought maybe I could help."

She wanted to believe that; in fact, she did. But she also couldn't help remembering Hugh's comment about Orrin. Maybe it was time to broach the subject of Orrin with her father, as well.

"That's very good of you," she said carefully. "Find anything?"

"Not really. But did you notice Dr. D. was the one to find Piers Marsden's horse the day he was killed?"

"Yes. Well, he wasn't a veterinarian at the time." Mel had been two years ahead of her in school and had been out on a date with Connie when he'd found the horse. In actuality, Connie had been the one who'd spotted Hugh's vehicle up on the ridge where the horse had come from. She'd testified that Mel had already ridden off to return the horse to the MP, so she'd raced to town to report her findings. Her concern, she'd stated, had been because everyone already knew about Noel's rape and how upset Hugh had been. "What's your point?"

"Only that Dr. Denver was also the one to help you the other day when someone shot at you."

Taylor grew slightly annoyed. "He's a vet, Orrin. He didn't intend to be there. He was coming back from a call on a patient. Technically Hugh was there, too."

Orrin blanched and sat back down. "Yes'm. I just thought it's interesting."

Shaking her head, Taylor went to collect her son.

The golden retriever pups turned out to be gorgeous, and naturally Kyle wanted the whole litter. Taylor convinced him to narrow his choice to two of the five, and while he struggled over his choices, and Mel took care of a patient, she went outside to radio Orrin that she was running a bit late. On her way into the office again, she spotted Connie Denver out back.

The Denvers lived in the back rooms of the big old house, and Connie had obviously been hanging the morning wash. But most of it remained in the basket, and she was pacing back and forth, her arms wrapped tightly beneath her breasts. The odd scene had Taylor approaching to see if she could help.

"Connie? Hi. Are you okay?" She hadn't heard anything the woman had been muttering to herself, but having also noticed that Mel seemed preoccupied and…sadder than usual, triggered her curiosity.

The woman froze and stared at her as if she'd materialized out of thin air. "I didn't see— You'll want Mel. Mel's in the office."

"Yes, I know. Kyle's inside to see about getting a pet. I saw you and wondered if anything was wrong."

"No."

The woman certainly didn't encourage warm feelings, but for Mel's sake Taylor tried again. "You don't seem well, Connie. You must know I'm very fond of you and Mel, and if there's anything I can do for you...I'm a good listener.''

"He doesn't like me to talk to his clients."

"Well, Kyle and I can't be considered clients, really, although I suppose Kyle will be after today." As she spoke, Taylor studied the woman's odd behavior. "Have you met my son yet?"

"N-no. I don't...get out much. Strangers make me... I'm shy."

Shy? She was turning into a kook. From day one with the fiasco about the cake, every time she'd seen the woman, she'd behaved strangely. But for Mel's sake, she wanted to try to get along.

"Kyle's only thirteen and likes anyone who likes animals," she said with a soft chuckle. "You wouldn't feel shy around him. Come on. Let me introduce you."

Connie took a step backward from her as though Taylor had come to arrest her. "No. I don't have to if I don't want to."

"Everything all right here?" Mel joined Kyle holding two chubby puppies that were trying to lick his face. "Honey, are you not feeling well again?"

"You promised me you'd help me," she whined in her little-girl voice that oddly fitted her fussy attire. "And you said we'd go for a ride."

Mel looked as though he would like to be anywhere on earth except where he was. Pink cheeked and thoroughly flustered, he went to his wife and led her to the back door. "I told you, dear, after my appointments. You haven't taken your medication, have you?"

"I hate it. It makes me sleepy, and I hate you for lying to me!"

Jerking free, she hurried into the house and locked the storm door behind herself. Then she stuck her tongue out at him and disappeared.

As Mel sighed and raked both hands through his hair,

Taylor bit her lip and motioned a wide-eyed Kyle to head toward the truck. When he was out of earshot, she said, "Forgive me if I'm speaking out of turn, but she's getting worse, Mel."

"Only when she doesn't take her medication. You know she's always been very sensitive and high-strung. She's been battling depression, too, and the less likely it is that we'll have children, the worse she gets."

"I'm so sorry."

He managed a brave smile. "No-no! Don't be. She's really a lovely girl. I just hate that you haven't had a chance to see her at her best yet." He clapped his hands together. "So, it looks as though young Kyle there's fixed up."

Following his lead, Taylor focused on her son and started to walk toward the truck, too. "I'll say. Are you sure we can't pay you something for these cuties?"

"Absolutely not. Finding them good homes is what matters. Just make sure you bring them in for their shots. I've given Kyle some papers that explains it all, but give a yell if you run into trouble."

Since he seemed as anxious for them to leave as Taylor was to get away from there, she echoed Kyle's thanks, assisted her son and new friends into the truck and they returned to her father's with Missy and Max.

"I feel terrible for him," she told her father a short time later, sharing the experience. He'd already been introduced to the pups, and Kyle had taken them out back to begin potty training them. "He tries to cover for her, but what's he going to do when she starts to run off his business?"

"Oh, I think people are fairly tolerant of the loose screws around here," Emmett replied with a wink. "What's a small town without its eccentrics? I've picked her up on the county road myself a time or two. There she'd be, all dressed up in her Sunday finest, purse over her arm, talking to herself and as happy as a baby in bubble bath."

"How sad. It's clear Mel loves her, too. He's so gentle and protective of her."

Emmett shrugged. "What else can he be? She's not bad enough to lock up. They seem content most of the time, just keep to themselves."

"And to think Orrin had decided Mel deserved to be put under the proverbial magnifying glass because he'd been out near the shooting site the day Piers died as well as when I was shot at." She quickly shared that story, too. "Can you believe it?"

"Nope. Mel was scared of Piers, remember? Didn't like him much, but that's because Piers took some little girl from him. What was her name...?"

Taylor snapped her fingers. "Janetta! Ted Posner's niece. You're right." She shook her head as she remembered that brief summer crush in Mel's senior year. "Too bad Janetta never came back to town. Maybe Mel would have had a second chance. Anyway, since we're on the subject of Orrin—" it felt ridiculous to bring it up "—where was he during the time of Piers's death? Hugh seemed to think he's as strange as Connie."

"Honey, get over it. Orrin's been a faithful friend for...well, almost as long as you've been gone."

"Yes, but where did he come from originally? Could he have been in the vicinity at the time?"

Her father's craggy face took on a stormy countenance and he slapped the file she'd left him onto the coffee table. "For the love of— No he wasn't in the area per se, and he hails semioriginally from a loony bin, okay? He'd been put there by his stepfather when he was a kid, just because he fought tooth and nail when the guy beat the hell out of him. The stepfather had enough pull to get him committed for eight years, and let me tell you, poor Orrin went through stuff you don't want to hear about. Chances are he would still be there if the place hadn't gone under a sudden change in administration where all the patients' files were reviewed. Once he got out he ran like hell, and he hasn't looked back since. All I can say is that it's a miracle he's stayed as sane as he is! Take it from me, he has more on the ball than eighty percent of the folks in this town—and if you breathe a word of my having told you this to him or anyone, I will fire you. Now can we drop the subject, please!''

It had been a long time since she'd heard her father speak so passionately about anything, and Taylor felt badly that she'd been the one to stir such feelings. ''Pop, I'm sorry. Truly. But I'm desperate here. I'm swimming in fog. Hugh needs help. I've gone through that file three times and I can't see anything to sink my teeth into. I was *there* and nothing in my memory stands out as odd or irregular. Forgive me?''

He made a guttural sound and squeezed the hand she'd set on his shoulder. ''Don't you think I sympathize with what you kids are going through? Across this country there are countless crimes in small towns like this one that never get resolved. I've had a great deal of time to think about that while sitting here.''

''You've been a wonderful friend to these people, Dad.''

''Yeah, a Sunday cop, that's what I've turned into. Good for nothing but escorting funeral processions and providing security for seasonal bazaars. You…*you* should take my job. You've got the experience and energy needed for what's required these days.''

''Listen, cowboy, this town's growing too big for only one cop. Besides, I don't plan on working fourteen-to six-teen-hour shifts, seven days a week for the rest of my life.'' Having said that, Taylor added quietly, ''Hugh and I are hoping to start over, Dad.''

''Tell me something I don't know.''

''Don't say anything to Kyle, okay? Hugh expects so much of himself and wants even more for us. He won't want to take any risks while these threats are going on.''

Her father nodded, picking at the edge of his cast. ''He

got a dirty deal, Gracie. I know it now. And it shows the size of his heart how he's explained to Kyle why he has to come here to see the boy.''

This was news. Taylor demanded, ''When did he do that?''

''This morning after you went off like the fox you are. Don't worry...the boy's fine about it. I don't know what happened after their talk last night, but your son's a different person than the peashooter who arrived here almost two weeks ago.''

Taking that as a high compliment, Taylor kissed her father's cheek.

''And I'll go through the damned file again and see what I can find,'' he added.

When Taylor left him, he was looking very pleased with his view of the world from the couch.

Nothing else of major import happened that day. The protesting phone calls dwindled down to a trickle that Orrin handled with impressive incompetence. Since her father's explanation, she'd been watching the man when time permitted, and was beginning to understand many things—and appreciate more.

Hugh came to dinner at the house. His mother still wasn't back, but she'd called the night before to announce she would return soon.

''Noel's mending,'' he told Taylor as she walked him to his truck very late. It turned out that his sister wanted away from her present environment, the memories proving too much. She'd accepted a similar position at an Albuquerque home, and Jane was driving with her to help her get settled.

''I expect Mother to call me in two days or so,'' Hugh said. ''Four at the most.''

Taylor knew what he was telling her, and she put on a strong front. ''Good for Noel. She deserves a chance to find someone as special as she is.'' From the way Hugh wrapped her in his arms, though, she knew he wasn't fooled for a second.

"She doesn't hate you any more than my mother does, Blue. They're only protecting the family they have left, just as you would. Give them time. They'll come around."

"Sure." She needed to change the subject, though. "I heard Tito and the Montez boys, and a few others on your street, came out to help you wash down the building and trailer today."

"Yeah. Go figure."

"Come on, Hugh. You would have done the same."

Hugh nodded, but his eyes showed worry. "That doesn't get Sandoval behind bars, though, does it?"

No, and it wouldn't, since Murdock Marsden had a neighboring rancher come forward and announce that Lew had been at the MP all evening the night of the fire. Since the rancher was someone who relied on Murdock for water, the announcement left a bad taste in everyone's mouth who saw through the ploy. It was even suggested that Hugh probably started the fire himself to collect on the insurance policy.

"What insurance policy?" Hugh muttered. "My mother dropped it two years ago because the premiums had been more than she could afford. They'd been going up every quarter, never mind that she'd never filed a claim—ever!"

Taylor ached for him. They'd had such a lovely evening sharing Lola's dinner, and for once Lola had agreed to join them. Afterward, Hugh had gone outside with Kyle and the pups for "cigar talk" her father called it jokingly. She hadn't minded being left behind too much because she really had wanted a chance to get to know Lola better. And it really had been fun listening to her father trying to impress Lola with his knowledge of TV talk show hosts. But now it was her and Hugh's mouse-hole speck of time...yet all there was left to do was hold him.

"Please don't lose control," she said, laying her head against his shoulder. "I know this is like a recurring nightmare, but there are cracks in the great Marsden machine this time. He won't get away with this kind of manipulation twice.''

Hugh had no comment to make to that, but had soothed himself by tilting her face up for a long good-night kiss.

When he raised his head again, his eyes radiated the sweetest longing. ''Come back to the store with me.''

''You're killing me,'' she replied, turning into his shoulder to hide from the temptation of him. ''It's already late, Hugh. Besides, Kyle expects the best of us.''

He grimaced. ''So does your father. He thinks I should already be making plans to make an honest woman of you.''

''I agree.''

Hugh's arms tightened around her. ''I want to, sweetheart. With all my heart. But I won't tie you to my problems.''

''And here I thought marriage vows read, 'For better or worse'.''

''Worse doesn't include immediately catastrophic. No, until I have something to offer, I won't taint your good family name with mine. In the meantime, though...'' He slipped his hands to her hips and, under the protection of darkness and the truck that separated them from the house, he moved her intimately against him. ''Remember whose heart you own.''

How was she likely to forget when he made her burn with the briefest look, and throb with need at the slightest rub of his hips against hers? Taylor sought his lips again and showed him that she understood—and that the condition worked both ways.

''That mouth,'' he muttered, awarding her lower lip a final love bite. ''I'd better get out of here before I embarrass myself. Dream of me, my Lady Blue.''

''Always,'' she whispered.

Ten

Every day that followed proved both a blessing and torment to Taylor. She was grateful that no new trouble or threats had come from the MP Ranch, and on the home front Kyle was growing more and more comfortable with Hugh, and because of the pups he had less time to complain about being bored. Although he was grounded anyway because of the incident with Madeline Yancy, she did warn him to avoid town for other reasons. She didn't want him exposed to any insensitive remarks that might be made regarding his paternity. But most important, now that everyone knew his connection to Hugh, they were afraid that made him a target for more dangerous threats.

As for Hugh, his misfortune with the fire had stirred the consciences of some of the old-timers in town, and like his business neighbors, they were beginning to be less hesitant about being seen waving or talking to him. The evening before his mother's return, he'd told her he'd even seen a modest increase in business. Taylor knew how much he hoped for some improvement there. He wouldn't in good conscience leave his mother and the business to pursue his own dreams unless he knew she could afford to hire someone to replace him.

Naturally, his mother's return meant they would lose their tiny oasis of privacy, such as it was. Because they didn't know when or where they would be together again, Taylor slipped away for a few hours to be with him that night.

As always their lovemaking reflected both the history that made them so comfortable with each other, and the excitement their individual sensuality triggered. From the moment she slipped through the warehouse door and Hugh locked it behind her, the air hummed with electricity, and there wasn't an instant when they weren't somehow touching.

"Four days," Hugh groaned, initiating a hot, hungry kiss even as his hands worked at her shirt buttons. "Do you know...how much...I ache?"

She'd known from their first elated hug that he'd been anticipating this since she'd phoned to tell him she could make it. Now she ran seductive fingers down the front flap of his jeans and cupped him gently. Her caress drew a deep moan and he immediately pressed himself into her hand.

"Ah, hell." Abandoning her shirt, he attacked her jeans. "Don't shoot me, sweetheart. But if I don't..."

He didn't have to say more. She understood his need and it matched her own desire. Barely halfway to the office, they had their clothes adjusted and he was lifting her onto a wooden bench.

Torn between laughter and begging for him to hurry, Taylor gasped. "Hugh, if I get splinters—"

"I'll take them out with my teeth. You'll like it so much it'll be our new favorite foreplay."

Laughing again, she drew him closer, only to push him away. "Wait!" Belatedly she fumbled with the shirt pocket bearing her badge. "Here," she said, handing him a foil packet.

"Bless you. Do you know how tough it is to walk into a store in this town and get these?"

"About as easy as buying a pregnancy kit. Next time try the rest rooms at the gas station—and why are we whispering?"

Giddy as children, they both tried to open the packet at once, only to send the thing shooting off into the darkness. Hugh groaned, then looked at her as if they'd missed the last lifeboat on a sinking ship.

"Do you have another?"

"No, I was out of change!"

He groaned again and pressed his hot and damp forehead to hers. "Blue..."

She couldn't stand it, either. She drew him closer. "It'll be all right," she whispered. It had to be. They were due a change in luck. In any case the look on Hugh's beloved face as he sank into her, and the sweet, sweet pleasure of being filled completely, made the risk, any risk with him worth it.

"Ah, babe."

"It's so good."

"Kiss me. I got this hard only thinking about that."

"Where was I kissing you?"

He sucked in a sharp breath. "Don't...tease."

"How about promises?"

"You're just wanting off this table."

"Uh-uh...I love feeling your heartbeat inside me."

"Blue..."

"Anywhere inside me."

"Hold on, sweetheart."

"Did I hurt you?"

Taylor stroked Hugh's hair, loving the weight of him now that they moved to the cot, loving his breath caressing her breast. "No."

"I felt the roughness coming on, and you felt so good—"

She took his hand and quickly, lightly bit his palm. "I liked it." That sometimes the memories of prison combined with the pleasure of having her in his arms created a desperation that bordered on savage didn't frighten her. "Don't you know by now everything you are, everything you do to me, is wonderful?"

The heat in his gaze was followed by a slow smile. "Want me to check you for splinters?"

It was good to laugh again, but better to see him smiling. "In a minute. This is wonderful, too, being quiet like this. To pretend..." No, she wouldn't ruin things by getting maudlin.

Hugh turned his face against her breastbone and breathed deeply, brushed his lips against her skin. "There has to be an end to the pretending. I want you and Kyle, and a home," he said, moving his lips lower to her abdomen. "I want another child."

Taylor closed her eyes, the images a torment.

"I'm sorry, love." Hugh rose over her, lifting her into his arms. "I didn't mean to make you sad."

"I'm getting greedy." She touched the bruise on his cheek. It was healing fast, but reminded her too much of the danger, the dangers, he faced. "I want all of that, too. And making love at dawn...to watch you shave...to pull into the driveway and see your truck already there..." She gripped his hand. "Hugh, what if we moved your mother's trailer to the property? This way she would be close and you wouldn't have to worry about her."

He shook his head. "She's not ready for that, Blue."

"If she knew how much I love you, she'd forgive me."

"She knows how much I love you, and she won't forgive you."

It hurt, but Taylor couldn't stand the thought of spending the rest of their time together brooding. She lifted her chin. "I'll get to her. I'll inundate her with illegitimate grandchildren. She'll beg you to marry me just so she can show her face in town."

Hugh's chest shook with soft laughter. "There's a novel idea. I'd believe you'd consider doing it, too."

"Consider?" She rolled onto her stomach. "Now you'd better check for splinters."

Taylor chuckled softly as she drove away from the feed store. She was glad that she'd been able to leave Hugh smiling. Worn out, but smiling. She wouldn't have trouble falling asleep, either, but she decided to take a circuitous route through town to make sure everything looked to be in order before heading for home.

She reached for the radio mike. "Unit One to Central. Over."

"Central....yawning. I mean over."

"Orrin, is this job getting too exciting for you?"

"I had burritos for dinner. They always make me sleepy. You're out later than usual tonight, Miz Taylor. Over."

Taylor shook her head, wondering if she would ever cure him of his formality. "The stars look almost touchable tonight. Thought I'd make a last run through town before turning in. How're things over there? Over."

"Everything's been quiet. Got a call about Unit Two. It should be ready for you by Monday they said. Over. Wait! Unover me a second. I almost forgot...Sheriff Trammell sent a fax to all communities in the county. He said there's been some reports of kids messing with headstones at area cemeteries. Over."

"It's a little early for Halloween pranks, isn't it? Over."

"Yeah, but football practice starts next week. Kids're always trying to intimidate the next town's team by putting a headstone in front of the other school's mascot. Bet you'll see Gwynn's Funeral Home taking in their sample stones until after Thanksgiving. It ain't easy getting RIP in black spray paint off marble and granite. Over."

Taylor laughed softly, not at the vandalism, but at the

fact that Orrin sounded so knowledgeable about the procedure. She was sorry she'd even begun to wonder about him, and was glad her father had finally shared his story with her. "I'll swing around by there to take a look and then turn in. You have a good evening, *compadre*. Over and out."

She made an S-turn through the residential section, finally backtracking to the church and cemetery. There were virtually no lights out here, save the one highlighting Mel's clinic sign next door and those lighting his front door, so Taylor slowed, prepared to turn on the side lamp because there was virtually no moonlight, either. However, the mound of white by the left edge of the cemetery required no illumination.

She knew the family name carved on the huge marble monument. Marsden. What she intended to find out was what had been dropped before it.

Parking, she took the flashlight from the glove compartment and started across the grass. She was sure she had to be seeing things, but the closer she got the more the mound looked like a person...a person lying there. Then she heard the eerie sound that had the fine hairs on her forearm and at the back of her neck rising.

Moaning. No, keening.

"Do you mind!"

Startled, Taylor swung the flashlight to her right—directly into Mel Denver's face. He grimaced and she immediately shut off the beam.

"Mel! What on earth...?"

Ignoring her, he ran to Piers Marsden's grave and hunkered beside his weeping wife.

"I've got this under control, Taylor."

She barely recognized his voice. It was harsh with anger...or was it bitterness, and not a little embarrassment. She could understand that well enough. What man wanted anyone to see that his wife preferred to lie over a corpse than beside him?

Speechless, she watched as he lifted the woman dressed in a flowing cotton gown-style nightshirt into his arms. Taylor was impressed. Connie wasn't bantam weight and Mel had never struck her as particularly strong. In fact, dressed in jeans, which from the looks of things he'd dragged on once realizing his wife was missing, she could see his pale torso seemed almost gaunt.

Without another word he carried his wife back to their house.

Taylor knew her mouth was open, but she couldn't help it. Connie and Piers? Piers with Connie?

Totally flabbergasted, she retraced her steps to the car. She needed to think about this. She needed to talk to her father.

Once she pulled into the driveway, however, she received her second shock of the evening. Lola's car was still in the driveway...and the house was virtually dark.

Things couldn't get any more mind jarring if they tried.

Okay, Lola and Dad as lovers is not a revelation. You know between his accident and your arrival it's probably put as much a crimp in their routine as Jane's return will put in yours and Hugh's.

But the timing for this wasn't convenient at all.

Parking so as not to block in Lola's candy apple red sedan, Taylor went inside. As she expected, the house was dark save the small lamp in the entryway that illuminated the stairs. She made her way quietly to her room, telling herself that it would be better to sleep on the matter, anyway. Connie Denver made Orrin Lint seem as sharp as a neurosurgeon; why should her behavior tonight seem so off the wall? If truth be known, Connie probably fixated about a great number of things. In the morning when she told her father about what she'd seen, he would undoubtedly come to the same conclusion.

Nevertheless, she tossed and turned all night, and when she finally did get to sleep, she had nightmares—nightmares where she combined the young boy who'd aimed the gun on her that horrible night and Mel. She heard herself scream, "No!" saw herself pull the trigger and then Mel—not the boy—Mel was flying backward...flying and flying. The whole scene happening in slow motion, his eyes already dead, his mouth shaped into the huge O of a silent scream.

Gasping, she sat up in bed. She was soaking wet and shaking like someone in the throes of malaria.

"God, help me," she moaned, covering her face with her trembling hands. She felt dizzy, her mind was so overloaded. But what did it all mean?

The room was still dark, but a hint of gray could be seen in the sky outside her open window. Checking the clock on the nightstand told her it was only 5:30 a.m. She turned off the alarm and decided to take her shower, anyway. There was no way she would go back to sleep again. Even if she could, she didn't want to think of what other torments her imagination would inflict on her.

It came as no surprise that she ached all over. Between the physical ecstasy that she'd shared with Hugh and the muscle-clenching horror she'd fabricated in her sleep, her body reacted as if she'd run a marathon.

The shower helped, but as she let herself out of the house, she accepted it had done nothing for her pounding headache. Wishing she'd taken some aspirin, she drove into town and saw that Lola's café was just opening. On impulse she pulled in.

She was grateful to be the first customer and that Lola's help was either busy in the kitchen or preoccupied with setting tables. That gave her the privacy to do what she wanted to do the instant she saw the older woman's worried expression. No, she amended, what she should have done for a long time.

Rounding the corner of the cash register counter she gave her father's lover a big bear hug.

"Oh, hon. I was so worried about what you'd think."

"I think you're terrific. And I think you should knock

on my head and see if anyone's home because I've been
selfish and self-preoccupied, and I hadn't given a thought
to your and Dad's relationship. Forgive me.''

"Sweetie, there's nothing to forgive. I'm nuts about
your daddy, but I learned a long time ago to appreciate
what he has to give and not ask for the moon.''

"Hmm. I think it's about time you stop selling yourself
short. If you'll pour me a cup of coffee and find me two
aspirin, I'll even donate my considerable abilities in co-
ercion. Dad was still asleep when I left the house so I
didn't want to make any noise in the kitchen.''

Lola nodded, her smile positively radiant. "Well, how
can I refuse an offer like that?''

When she left the café twenty minutes later, she still felt
exhausted, but her headache was easing, helped not only
by the aspirin, but by the better communication between
her and the woman she wouldn't mind at all being her
stepmother.

After checking in at the station, she wanted desperately
to stop by and share last night's revelation with Hugh. But
he'd warned her that he would be leaving for Albuquerque
before dawn in order to get back before missing too much
of the business day. She missed him all the more when
Mel phoned the station looking for her.

Taylor signaled Orrin to say she was out and that he
would pass on the message. When Orrin hung up, he gave
her a quizzical look.

"Something wrong?''

"Let's put it this way—something's definitely not
right.'' She checked her watch; it was shortly after nine
o'clock. "Do me a favor and phone the chief for me. Tell
him I'm on my way home, that I need to talk to him.''

Preoccupied, she left the station and climbed into the
Blazer. As a result, when the woman huddling low on the
back seat sat up and appeared in the rearview mirror, Taylor couldn't quite repress a sharp gasp.

"Good morning, Taylor. I didn't mean to startle you.''

Connie Denver sat in the middle of the back seat, dressed in one of her prettier floral print dresses with the inevitable lace collar and shortsleeved cuffs. She held a matching pink bag on her lap, and looked, Taylor thought, as if she was either going to church or high tea.

"People who don't mean to startle people don't hide in the back seat of their vehicles, Connie."

"It couldn't be helped. I had to talk to you, but I didn't want to be seen."

"All right, what seems to be the problem?"

"Could we get away from traffic? I mean it—I can't be seen."

Taylor didn't like being put in this situation at all, but since the woman hadn't made any threats yet, did in fact seem more rational than she had been since Taylor had returned to Redoubt, she felt compelled to start the Blazer and head toward the parking lot exit.

"Which way?"

"Right."

"You want me to take you home?"

"No!" Connie reached over the seat and gripped her arm. "I won't go back. You can't make me."

Whatever confidence Taylor had felt about the situation, it vanished at that outburst. She did, however, make a right turn as the woman directed.

"No one's going to make you do anything you don't want, Connie. Take a deep breath and start from the beginning. What's got you upset and why don't you want to go home to Mel?"

Connie settled back in her seat and said matter-of-factly, "Because he would stop us. He doesn't want anyone to know. But it's time."

Taylor kept her head straightforward, but her gaze busily scanned the area. Where was everyone? It was part of the busiest time of the day and yet they passed no car. There was no one strolling on the sidewalk.

"Time for what?"

"Justice."

Taylor wet lips that had gone suddenly dry. Was she admitting that Mel was the one they had been looking for all this time? Mel killed Piers?

"Central to Unit One. Over."

As Orrin's voice broke her introspection, she reached for the speaker, but Connie sprang forward to grab her wrist. The strength in her fingers surprised Taylor.

"There's no time," she said.

"If I don't respond to Orrin, he'll wonder that something's wrong, Connie."

"I said no!" In an angry and unexpected move, the woman snatched the mike and jerked it from the radio, then flung the thing onto the floorboard by her feet.

Taylor's heart began to pound.

"Okay," she drawled, attempting to sound conversational. She turned off the set completely. "No more radio. Why don't you talk to me instead. Am I going the right way? Do you want me to turn soon?"

"Why are you pretending not to know?"

Taylor glanced into the rearview mirror and saw Connie's disapproving stare. "I'm not pretending. I understand you're really upset about something, and I know you want me to head toward the mountains, don't you? But why, Connie? Do you want to show me a secret?"

"Yes, a secret."

"And you're afraid Mel wouldn't want you to tell?"

"He would hurt you if you did. He loves me."

"I know he does. He showed it again last night, didn't he? When he found you at Piers's grave and he carried you home?"

"You were there. It worried him."

"He said that?"

"He didn't have to. We understand each other completely."

Taylor finally saw a vehicle approaching her. Not just any vehicle.

"Exactly what do you two understand, Connie?"

"Why we did what we had to do..."

Connie opened her purse, which drew Taylor's gaze to the mirror again. She watched in growing dread as the woman drew out a small handgun.

"Why we'll always do what we have to do..."

As Hugh's truck drew nearer, she saw him break into a smile and wave. It took all her willpower not to react. Not to hit the brakes, and hope to heaven that she could disarm Connie before she hurt anyone.

She saw his confusion, almost felt his shock, his unease, and she prayed that he would react as she needed him to react.

"It won't matter, you know."

"What won't?"

"He won't be able to help you. Just like he didn't help Piers."

That confused Taylor. "How could he? He and Piers fought and Hugh left. Was Mel watching, Connie?" she asked, taking a blind reach. "Was he jealous that you wanted Piers? You were dating him? Both of them?"

"I was true. Always true."

But that didn't add up. "Piers could never be. With him it was the more the merrier."

"He couldn't help himself. They flirted with him."

"Noel didn't flirt with Piers, Connie. She was afraid of him and his temper."

"No! She wanted him the same way I did. They all did. Turn here..."

Taylor intended to keep going. She could see no one approaching in her rearview mirror. Hugh hadn't understood, and that meant she had to try to continue driving until somehow she figured out a way—

She gasped in excruciating pain as Connie grabbed a fistful of her hair and pressed the gun to her head.

"Turn!"

Tears blurring her vision from the sting of her hair being

tugged out by the roots, Taylor made the turn up the road that led to the bluff. Once Connie got what she wanted, she released her and grew almost sedate again.

Taylor adjusted her grip on the steering wheel and took several deep breaths to compose herself. Her rage toward this woman was building, but she knew if her emotions got out of control, she would lose.

"Piers felt more for Noel, didn't he?" she began her intellectual attack again. "That's why even though he had to resort to rape to get her, you saw it as the ultimate betrayal."

"He promised me it was over. He was supposed to be mine forever. But because of her, the police would be coming. The police would take him away and then we couldn't get married."

"So you shot Piers to keep him for yourself..." It was the only explanation. The testimony that she'd given at Hugh's trial had to be more lies.

Connie frowned. "No. Mel did it. He did it for me because he loved me."

Taylor stopped at the bluff where it had all happened. She looked out at the rolling hills and pictured that day.

"I don't think so. I don't think that's what happened at all." Taylor turned as much as her seat belt allowed her. "You followed Hugh up here. You knew why he was coming for Piers. He would have gone straight to the house if necessary, he was that angry, but he spotted Piers riding up here and he came up...and you followed. Where did you leave your car? Where did you hide?"

"It doesn't matter. Get out now. No—not that hand," she said as Taylor reached for her seat belt with her right. "The other one."

When they were out of the truck, Connie motioned her forward. "And keep your hands up."

"Tell me the rest, Connie," Taylor said. She took the smallest steps she thought she could get away with. "After you shot Piers—"

"No. Why do you keep saying that? Mel did it. And then he took the gun—"

"How could he take the gun when he already had it?"

"You're trying to confuse me."

"No, I'm not. He wasn't even here."

"He came because he saw me from the road."

So part of the testimony had been true. Just altered to protect Connie—and to frame Hugh. "And after you shot Piers, he took the gun and he planted it in Hugh's truck," Taylor said, heartsick all over again.

"He didn't want them to take me because he loved me, and was going to take care of me from then on." She frowned again. "He did, too. Too well. I didn't like going to the doctor, but he said it was necessary."

Taylor froze. "What...?"

"It hurt. And then I could never have another baby, but I didn't want another one. I wanted mine."

Dear heaven, this was the most wretched story. She'd always known Connie had come from a rigid and dysfunctional family, but how bad could it have been that it had set her on this course? As she looked down the short barrel of the gun pointed at her, she knew she was running out of time. "You know you can't use that," she told her. "People saw us together as we drove up here. They'll know."

"Who? A convict and a convict's mother? No. They'll find you broken at the bottom of the cliffs. Everyone knew how you wouldn't leave things alone. Always poking into things, being where you shouldn't be. Mel will tell me what I should say. He's going to be angry with me, but he'll know what I should say."

"Not this time, lady. Not even Mel can lie you out of this mess." And Taylor thought if she was to die, at least she could take satisfaction in that the story would at last come out. "Will you tell me one more thing?" she asked as Connie approached, forcing her to back to the very edge of the bluff where Piers had been found. "Did you shoot at my car the day I talked to Lew Sandoval up here?"

"No. Mel saw you. He thought it was a lucky break, that it would make you suspect Lew. If Lew had to die later, that would be all right. Nobody would miss him."

"Good Lord, how many people were you willing to kill!"

"We were in trouble," she said, her expression blank, as if she didn't understand how anyone could ask such an obvious question. "We had to help Mr. Marsden make you go away."

"So you started the fire at the feed store, wanting us to think Murdock Marsden was behind it."

"But Mel helped put it out, too. Now when Hugh finds he's lost you, he'll blame Mr. Marsden. He'll get himself sent back to prison, and we'll be safe again."

Taylor shook her head. "You've forgotten my father, Connie. He won't buy any of that. He'll investigate and he'll find out about you, about how unwell you are. And you know what they'll do? They'll take you away, not Hugh. Mel can't take care of you anymore, Connie. He'll be going to jail, too. He's been an accessory to murder, an accessory to assault on a police officer, he's committed arson... You'll never see each other again."

"Stop it!" Connie aimed.

Taylor didn't think, she threw herself over the side of the cliff.

She rolled and rolled, vaguely aware of shots ringing out. If any struck her, she couldn't tell; the sharp rocks and brush were doing their own damage.

Suddenly she slammed into something that wouldn't give. Agonizing pain shot through her head and back. Her breath was knocked out of her lungs and the world went black like a camera shutter that closes and never reopens.

Eleven

"Taylor...*Blue,* can you hear me?"

She didn't want to open her eyes. She had a feeling doing so would hurt more than she already did. Grimacing, she reached for her head.

"Don't! Don't move a muscle. You might bust that shrubbery loose."

Her heart filled with joy at the sound of Hugh's voice. But as some of her confusion and dizziness faded, she remembered Connie.

"That's it, sweetheart. I'm coming down to get you."

"Wait...she's...gun!"

The words wouldn't come out right, and as she tried to open her eyes, the sun's glare blinded her.

"Everything's under control, Gracie," her father yelled. "You listen to Hugh now."

She knew she had to be hallucinating. Her father was home with a broken leg. Then she heard more voices, some that sounded more familiar than others. She thought Jer

Trammell's was among them, but when she felt dirt and rocks pelt her, she opened her eyes again and saw only Hugh. Big, beautiful Hugh Thomas Blackstone rappelling down the slope. She'd never seen a more glorious sight in her life.

"Almost there, love. Hang on."

"I'm not going anywhere."

"That's the spirit. How do you feel?"

"Like I jumped off a cliff. Where is she?"

"Don't you worry about her. Trammell's people have her secured. Let's concentrate on you." He blotted out the sun as he hovered over her. Gently caressing her cheek, he scanned her from head to foot. "My poor Blue...can you tell if you've been shot?"

"I don't think so."

"I see blood on your head and coming through the tear on your thigh."

"I think I'm okay. I know I love you."

To her amazement she saw tears fill his eyes.

"And I love you. Want to get out of here and discuss what we should do about it?"

"The sooner the better."

He tied the second line he'd brought down to her waist and helped her to her feet. More dizziness and nausea had her clutching at him, but he was more solid than the mountain they were balanced on.

"Easy. Don't try too much all at once."

"I could fly out of here if you'd just kiss me."

"You'll never have to ask me twice," he murmured, brushing a tender kiss across her dust-coated lips.

"Hey, you two." Her father tugged at the ropes. "Save it for better ground. Riley! Start 'er forward. Slow!"

The ropes that had been tied to a deputy sheriff's car made it easy for Taylor and Hugh to reach the top again. Once they were standing under their own power, Hugh wrapped his arms around her for real.

She gasped and clutched her side. "Uh-oh. I may have cracked something, after all."

Whispering what sounded like a prayer, Hugh carefully lifted her into his arms.

"I said my ribs, Blackstone, not my feet. Hiya, Pop. What are you doing on that leg?"

"Did you think I was going to just sit at the house and wait for the phone to ring?" he snapped. But his eyes, too, were overbright, and his hand shook as he touched her hair.

Hugh began walking toward his truck. "I was so damned afraid," he said, his voice exposing some lingering dread. "When I saw that look on your face as I passed you, and then I saw her in the truck...I knew. I just knew."

"I hoped you would. So you went and told Dad?"

"Who called for reinforcements while I drove. Mother's with Kyle, by the way. You can use the cellular when I get you into the truck. He was pretty shaken when we left him."

"Then I'm glad he has your mother," Taylor replied, not allowing her personal problems with the woman to offset what was good for her son. "And who knows—maybe this is the start of a good thing."

Hugh smiled. "I think she's going to come around pretty quickly now, sweetheart."

As he set her in the truck and Jer Trammell came over to shake her hand, she filled him in on everything she knew of the bizarre story.

"I'll have one of my boys get Denver right now," the stern-faced cop said once she finished. He immediately beckoned to one of his men. "As for Mardsen, I'm going to enjoy filling him in on what a big mistake he made."

"I'd like to go with you," Hugh said.

Taylor immediately took hold of his hand. "Oh, no, cowboy. If I have to go to the hospital, you're going with me."

The grim intent in his eyes melted into tenderness the

moment he met her entreating gaze, and his grip on her hand tightened. "What was I thinking? You're absolutely right, love. We've been apart long enough."

And then not caring that they had a dozen eyes on them, he swooped into the cab and kissed her for real.

In the weeks that followed, Connie Denver was found unfit to stand trial for the murder of Piers Marsden and was committed to a psychiatric facility in Albuquerque. Mel was arraigned and scheduled to stand trial for his part in the crimes next month.

Lew Sandoval was threatened with prosecution for his various infractions and offenses, and voluntarily left the county. As for Murdock Marsden, he'd neither apologized to Hugh—something that offended Taylor greatly—nor had he been seen in public since Jer Trammel's visit to the MP, a condition she did support.

She and Hugh were married on the first Saturday in October in the town church with just immediate family in attendance. That included, of course, Lola and Orrin. Jane proved the most sentimental, sniffing throughout the ceremony. Once she'd been informed of the entire story, she'd shown a great capacity for forgiveness and had apologized in many ways to Taylor, the most welcome that she was proving a warm and encouraging grandmother to Kyle.

As for Noel, she phoned several times but didn't return for the ceremony. Taylor understood and she assured her that the elegant anniversary glasses she'd sent as a gift would be their most cherished and used present.

After the ceremony she and Hugh drove to her father's house, wanting to change so they could be as comfortable as the rest of the locals who'd accepted Lola's invitation to a wedding reception at the café. As Taylor paused before the dresser mirror and removed the wreath of flowers from her hair, she watched Hugh slip out of his suit jacket and tug off his tie. In the process he stopped to look at his ring and smile.

"I love looking at mine, too," she told him softly.

He crossed to her and kissed the back of her head, his gaze holding hers in the mirror as he lowered the zipper of the sheath that perfectly matched her eyes. "Did you think anyone will notice if we're late?"

"I think they'll be shocked if we're not." And she sighed out of sheer bliss as he smoothed the dress off her shoulders and traced the lacy border of the demi-bra that was also a shimmering sky blue.

"I don't think I've ever seen you look lovelier," he murmured, kissing the side of her neck. "Glowing." Then he unhooked the bra and peeled it off, leaving her only in sexy lace panty hose and heels. "But I like you best like this."

Laughing throatily, Taylor turned into his arms and reached into his pants pocket. Earlier they'd placed a foil packet in there. Their "something new" to fulfill wedding tradition, she'd teased. "Well, in that case," she murmured, tossing the packet over her shoulder, "I like you best like *this*."

Hugh grew still, and his eyes radiated a passion he saved only for her. "You're sure? You don't mind not waiting?"

Oh, they had discussed it when they'd first learned she wasn't pregnant yet. But she'd seen his disappointment, and as one by one the stumbling blocks had lifted out of their way—most recently that his conviction had been overturned and that he would soon be taking the bar exam—she decided she could think of nothing else that would put this look in his eyes.

"Waiting for what?" she murmured, backing him to the bed. "To be sure that I love you? To be sure that you love me? To be sure we've been blessed?" she concluded as he sat down.

His expression grew sober, his hands gentle but the hold unbreakable as he drew her to him. "Then come to me, Lady Blue. Love me."

"Be my dream and I'll be yours," she whispered against his lips.

Those were their real vows, she thought as his strong arms closed around her. And this was their beginning.

* * * * *

Daniel MacGregor is at it again…

New York Times bestselling author

NORA ROBERTS

introduces us to a new generation of MacGregors
as the lovable patriarch of the illustrious MacGregor
clan plays matchmaker again, this time to his three
gorgeous granddaughters in

THE MACGREGOR BRIDES

From Silhouette Books

Don't miss this brand-new continuation of Nora Roberts's
enormously popular *MacGregor* miniseries.

Available November 1997 at your favorite retail outlet.

▼ Silhouette®

Look us up on-line at: http://www.romance.net

NRMB-S

SHARON SALA

Continues the twelve-book series—36 HOURS— in October 1997 with Book Four

FOR HER EYES ONLY

The storm was over. The mayor was dead. Jessica Hanson had an aching head...and sinister visions of murder. And only one man was willing to take her seriously— Detective Stone Richardson. He knew that unlocking Jessica's secrets would put him in danger, but the rugged cop had never expected to fall for her, too. Danger he could handle. But love...?

For Stone and Jessica and *all* the residents of Grand Springs, Colorado, the storm-induced blackout was just the beginning of 36 Hours that changed *everything!* You won't want to miss a single book.

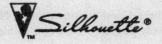

Look us up on-line at: http://www.romance.net

36HRS4

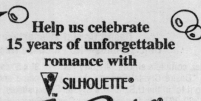

**Help us celebrate
15 years of unforgettable
romance with**

SILHOUETTE®

Desire®

You could win a genuine lead crystal vase, or one of 4 sets of 4 crystal champagne flutes! Every prize is made of hand-blown, hand-cut crystal, with each process handled by master craftsmen. We're making these fantastic gifts available to be won by you, just for helping us celebrate 15 years of the best romance reading around!

DESIRE CRYSTAL SWEEPSTAKES
OFFICIAL ENTRY FORM

To enter, complete an Official Entry Form or 3" x 5" card by hand printing the words "Desire Crystal Sweepstakes," your name and address thereon and mailing it to: in the U.S., Desire Crystal Sweepstakes, P.O. Box 9076, Buffalo, NY 14269-9076; in Canada, Desire Crystal Sweepstakes, P.O. Box 637, Fort Erie, Ontario L2A 5X3. Limit: one entry per envelope, one prize to an individual, family or organization. Entries must be sent via first-class mail and be received no later than 12/31/97. No responsibility is assumed for lost, late, misdirected or nondelivered mail.

DESIRE CRYSTAL SWEEPSTAKES
OFFICIAL ENTRY FORM

Name: _____

Address: _____

City: _____

State/Prov.: _____ Zip/Postal Code: _____

KFO

15YRENTRY

Desire Crystal Sweepstakes
Official Rules—No Purchase Necessary

To enter, complete an Official Entry Form or 3" x 5" card by hand printing the words "Desire Crystal Sweepstakes," your name and address thereon and mailing it to: in the U.S., Desire Crystal Sweepstakes, P.O. Box 9076, Buffalo, NY 14269-9076; in Canada, Desire Crystal Sweepstakes, P.O. Box 637, Fort Erie, Ontario L2A 5X3. Limit: one entry per envelope, one prize to an individual, family or organization. Entries must be sent via first-class mail and be received no later than 12/31/97. No responsibility is assumed for lost, late, misdirected or nondelivered mail.

Winners will be selected in random drawings (to be conducted no later than 1/31/98) from among all eligible entries received by D. L. Blair, Inc., an independent judging organization whose decisions are final. The prizes and their approximate values are: Grand Prize—a Mikasa Crystal Vase ($140 U.S.); 4 Second Prizes—a set of 4 Mikasa Crystal Champagne Flutes ($50 U.S. each set).

Sweepstakes offer is open only to residents of the U.S. (except Puerto Rico) and Canada who are 18 years of age or older, except employees and immediate family members of Harlequin Enterprises, Ltd., their affiliates, subsidiaries and all other agencies, entities and persons connected with the use, marketing or conduct of this sweepstakes. All applicable laws and regulations apply. Offer void wherever prohibited by law. Taxes and/or duties on prizes are the sole responsibility of the winners. Any litigation within the province of Quebec respecting the conduct and awarding of a prize in this sweepstakes may be submitted to the Régie des alcools, des courses et des jeux. All prizes will be awarded; winners will be notified by mail. No substitution for prizes is permitted. Odds of winning are dependent upon the number of eligible entries received.

Any prize or prize notification returned as undeliverable may result in the awarding of that prize to an alternative winner. By acceptance of their prize, winners consent to use of their names, photographs or likenesses for purposes of advertising, trade and promotion on behalf of Harlequin Enterprises, Ltd., without further compensation unless prohibited by law. In order to win a prize, residents of Canada will be required to correctly answer a time-limited, arithmetical skill-testing question administered by mail.

For a list of winners (available after January 31, 1998), send a separate stamped, self-addressed envelope to: Desire Crystal Sweepstakes 5309 Winners, P.O. Box 4200, Blair, NE 68009-4200, U.S.A.

Sweepstakes sponsored by Harlequin Enterprises Ltd., P.O. Box 9042, Buffalo, NY 14269-9042.

At last the wait is over....

ANN
MAJOR

brings us two brand-new titles in her series

CHILDREN OF DESTINY
When Passion and Fate Intertwine...

From Silhouette Desire in November 1997—
NOBODY'S CHILD
Man of the Month Cutter Lord didn't want the familiar,
reckless passion he felt for ex-flame Cheyenne Rose to
come rushing back. But once he stumbled upon her
secret—their son—he wouldn't let her go.

And available as a Silhouette Single Title
in February 1998—
SECRET CHILD
Although everyone told Jack West that his wife,
Chantal—the woman who'd betrayed him and sent him to
prison for a crime he didn't commit—had died, Jack
knew she'd merely transformed herself into supermodel
Mischief Jones. But when he finally captured the woman
he'd been hunting, could he really believe she was an
innocent pawn in a dark conspiracy?

"Want it all? Read Ann Major."
—Nora Roberts, *New York Times* Bestselling Author

Don't miss these wonderful books, available at your
favorite retail outlet. Only from Silhouette Books.

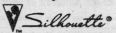

SILHOUETTE WOMEN KNOW ROMANCE WHEN THEY SEE IT.

And they'll see it on **ROMANCE CLASSICS**, the new 24-hour TV channel devoted to romantic movies and original programs like the special **Romantically Speaking—Harlequin™ Goes Prime Time.**

Romantically Speaking—Harlequin™ Goes Prime Time introduces you to many of your favorite romance authors in a program developed exclusively for Harlequin® and Silhouette® readers.

Watch for **Romantically Speaking—Harlequin™ Goes Prime Time** beginning in the summer of 1997.

If you're not receiving ROMANCE CLASSICS, call your local cable operator or satellite provider and ask for it today!

Escape to the network of your dreams.

See Ingrid Bergman and Gregory Peck in *Spellbound* on Romance Classics.

©1997 American Movie Classics Co. "Romance Classics" is a service mark of American Movie Classics Co.
Harlequin is a trademark of Harlequin Enterprises Ltd.
Silhouette is a registered trademark of Harlequin Books, S.A.

RMCLS-S-R2